# God's Tin Soldiers

2009 11 01   18:15

# God's Tin Soldiers

### D Montgomery MacLean

First edition 2009
Revised first edition 2009
Second edition 2009

MONMAC  Publishing,  Stockholm
ISBN  978-91-633-4297-4

In loving memory of

Richard Bean McLean

# *Contents*

# *Preface*

*Ships that pass in the night and speak each other in passing;*
*Only a signal shown and a distant voice in the darkness;*
*So on the ocean of life we pass and speak one another,*
*Only a look and a voice; then darkness again and a silence.*

Henry Wadsworth Longfellow

When a believer and a non-believer discuss religion, it is usually like two ships passing in the night. They are aware of each other's presence; they speak to one another; but they continue on their respective ways unaffected by the meeting.

Each is convinced that the other is misguided and that his or her views can therefore be dismissed with disdain. That is the way it might have been between the two young people at the centre of this story, had it not been for one thing: John is in love with Yvette.

Only by treating Yvette's belief with respect, does John stand any chance of dissuading her from her determination to become a nun. What he does is basically to say "OK. Let's assume that everything the Bible says is correct. How can we then explain these observable facts, which appear to contradict the Bible?" He tries to say it, of course, in a more imaginative—and humorous—way. In the course of doing so, John comes up with several intriguing new ideas.

Yvette's response shows that hers is not a blind, unthinking belief. Nor is it devoid of humour.

The notes at the back of the book are in no way essential to the understanding or enjoyment of this story. They are provided solely for the benefit of those unfortunate souls (the author must sheepishly confess to being amongst their number) who are unable to relax until they have checked out the facts for themselves. The hope is that instead of sitting uncomfortably amidst tottering piles of opened reference books, such readers will be able to retreat to their hammocks, or perhaps sink down into a warm bath, and do their research by flipping to the back of the book—not forgetting to hold their place in the narrative with their left thumb.

If you number yourself amongst the fact-checkers, please consider enjoying the story first and doing your fact checking afterwards—or at least waiting until you get to the end of a chapter. To make this easier to do, each note is preceded by the original context and the number of the page on which it occurs. Footnotes have been deliberately avoided in the text, so as not to interrupt the flow of the narrative.

D Montgomery MacLean
September 2009

# Chapter 1

## *The Drive From Montreal*

All men are not born equal. Neither are all women. Some are beautiful; some are not. Some are superbly fitted-out in the brain dept; others less so. Yvette Dumont had come out a winner on both counts. But she was going to throw it all away. She had decided to become a nun.

Although these thoughts featured prominently in John Cunningham's mind as he turned off the main road from Montreal to the Eastern Townships, they were not at the forefront. That region of his mind was focused on the intense whiteness that was all he could see through the incessant swishing of the windscreen wipers. The road was white. The trees were white. And the snow which flew straight at them was glisteningly white. By blinking, and looking slightly to one side, he could just make out the ruts in the road made by a car somewhere ahead of them.

They had been forced to open the triangular vent windows a notch to keep the mist from building up on the windscreen. The resulting noise almost drowned out the music from the car radio, which the small group of grey cells that had not been placed on emergency alert suggested might be one of Mozart's divertimenti. Did it matter at this point? John felt that it did. If they were going to fly off the road, and perhaps leave this world altogether, then he wanted to do it to heavenly music.

He knew that Yvette felt the same way. A love of beautiful music was one of the things that had drawn them together in the first place. When Yvette had flipped through the stations on the car radio, most of which were blaring out Elvis Presley, Everly Bros, and suchlike, and had come to one playing Beethoven's violin concerto, she didn't have to ask John if she should stop there.

From Yvette's point of view, they were in what a management consultant would call a "win-win" situation: Beethoven and Mozart in this world and—if they wrapped themselves around a telephone pole—choruses of angels in the next. John was less convinced about the certainty of the second outcome, and even if it were to turn out to be so, he was not at all sure that he wanted to spend eternity listening to angels singing. As if to underline his scepticism, he slowed down a bit more.

However, what mattered right now was that Yvette was utterly convinced that angels and all things Godly were of paramount importance, and that her duty was to devote her life to their service. That was why they were travelling to the Cunningham's cottage on Lake Gomareph.

Although situated on the lake, the cottage was not far from a ski hill, which is where John had met Yvette when they were both still in high school. She had come with her school class on a day trip, and by chance they had travelled up together on the ski lift.

This had led to their going out together for a couple of years, until John became aware that, fond as he was of Yvette, they had diametrically opposed ideas about the purpose of youth. Yvette felt they should be planning for their future together, whereas John wanted to see the world. The deciding moment had come when Yvette asked him if he didn't long to hear the patter of little feet, and John realized that he did not. Not little feet; not mortgages; not a 9-to-5 job; not any aspect of family life. He wanted freedom and no responsibility.

So he had broken off their relationship. Brutally. He could remember feeling quite sophisticated at the time. Yvette had been devastated, but after all, men of the world had to take such things in their stride. Now the tables were turned.

John recalled his grandfather likening the French and English communities in Quebec to a busy train station during morning rush hour: thousands of people in close proximity crossing one another's paths, but with very little interaction. John had not seen Yvette since they split up. Although he and Yvette had, of course, met some of each others friends, once they had separated these ties between their two worlds withered away for want of use—until just before Christmas when John had been invited to a dinner party by one of Yvette's friends.

He realized now that her friends must have hoped that meeting John again might cause Yvette to have second thoughts about abandoning the pleasures of this world for a cold cell in a convent and a promise of better things in the world to come. However, this plan did not seem to have worked. Yvette was just as determined as ever. Instead, it was John who was having the second thoughts. And third, and fourth as well.

They pulled off onto the winding road that ran parallel to the lake. By the look of things, a plough had been along more than once today, and had thrown up high walls of snow on both sides of the road. However, the snow was already building up again and there were two deep ruts in the centre of the road. John hoped that Pierre had been to the cottage and cleared off their drive.

Another thing John hoped was that he would not meet someone travelling in the opposite direction. The road was barely wide enough at the best of times for two cars to squeeze past one another at slow speed, and this was not the best of times.

As it turned out, they did meet a black pick-up, with a plough mounted on the front of it, coming towards them. But it saw John coming, took a quick swipe with its plough at someone's drive, and pulled off the road. As they drew closer, John recognized Pierre, who rolled down his window to tell them that he had just cleared off their drive for the second time. John shouted his thanks and drove on.

It would have been impossible for the Cunninghams to use their cottage year round as they did without Pierre Laporte's help. In fact, this side of Lake Gomareph was almost a Laporte family business. In addition to ploughing snow and supplying firewood for many of the families along the lake, which Pierre did himself, his wife Nicole did housecleaning and laundry. During the summer months, when school was out, their children helped out with everything from mowing lawns to repairing docks and removing hornets' nests.

Just as Pierre had promised, when they reached their drive, which went quite steeply down from the road to the house, it had been neatly ploughed off. However, John decided not to drive down. The snowfall showed no sign of letting up, and he didn't want to have to call Pierre later to come and tow them up the drive. Instead, he pulled in to the spare parking space at the top of the drive, which Pierre had also ploughed off, and from where, if necessary, he could shovel the car out.

For almost the first time since leaving Montreal, John was able to let his gaze dwell on the girl who, in a week's time, was due to walk through the portals of Ste Marie d'en Haut convent and leave the world behind her. She wore no trace of make-up. But neither did she need to. Her blue eyes—royal blue was the colour that John had long ago decided they were—seemed to contain a hint of good-natured mischief, as if she had a water pistol in her pocket. Her lips were elegantly thin, quite unlike those bloated labial protrusions that Hollywood is so fond of. She had just covered her auburn hair with a fur cap, so that only a pony tail stuck out.

John had no difficulty understanding what had attracted him to her in the first place. In fact, his difficulty at this point lay in reminding himself of his reasons for breaking off their relationship.

His thoughts were interrupted at this juncture by a loud thumping on the port beam, which he recognized as coming from Lord Ronald, a six-year old golden retriever who had been so named after one of Stephen Leacock's characters—the one who flung himself upon his horse and rode madly off in all directions. As a young puppy, Lord Ronald, or Ron as he was affectionately known, had tried to join them one day when they were skating on the lake. His legs had taken off, if not in all directions, at least in four of them. It was Ron's tail which was now thumping the side of the car in a welcoming gesture.

John opened the door, and Ron allowed himself to be scratched behind the ears. But only for a moment. The door had opened on the other side of the car and that required immediate investigation.

"Hello, you yellow meatball" said Yvette affectionately, as Ron wriggled and whined and wagged his tail in excitement at seeing an old friend again after such a long absence—about forty years in canine time, not that Ron was much of a mathematician. He was too well behaved to jump up on Yvette without an invitation. However, the contortions of his body left no doubt that this is exactly what he would like to do.

"Allo, Yvette! Comment ça va?" Sarah, John's younger sister, had just arrived with the toboggan in tow, so that they would not have to risk life and limb carrying their suitcases and boxes of provisions down the driveway.

"Hello, Sarah! How are you?" Yvette and Sarah had enjoyed each other's company when Yvette and John were dating. Sarah had sometimes practiced her French with Yvette. But it usually didn't last very long. As was often the case in middle-class French-Canadian families, Yvette had been brought up bilingual, whereas Sarah had only her school French, which was fine for reading Victor Hugo, but was not much help when two high-spirited girls wanted to discuss a Victor or a Hugo they had met at a party.

"Hello, stranger!" Andrew, the youngest of the Cunningham siblings, hugged Yvette in a way that he probably would have hesitated to do next week, if he had met her wearing her habit. And Yvette would probably not have hugged him back that way either! thought John to himself as he opened the trunk of the car.

"How was the trip?" Andrew asked his brother.

"Sheer pleasure to start with: light snowfall in a bucolic landscape. We had a great time, listening to music and reminding each other of the things we had done together long ago. But just before we reached Granby, the snow started in earnest."

Their attention was diverted at this point. Golden retrievers are not yappy dogs. They are the strong, silent type, and do not bark at trivialities. But Ron was barking now. The Cunningham siblings looked up to see a presumptive nun, half-way down the drive on the toboggan, with a golden retriever in full pursuit. She stuck out her left foot and negotiated the sharp turn at the bottom, covering her surprised canine pursuer in a shower of snow. This manoeuvre brought her to a halt about three inches— although Yvette would probably have said it was all of 10 *centimètres*—from a somewhat startled Mrs Mary Cunningham.

"Hullo, Yvette, dear. Good to see you again." Mrs Cunningham had brought up four boisterous children and wasn't going to let herself be fazed by a near miss with a toboggan.

"Hello, Mrs Cunningham. You're looking very well!" Yvette meant every word of it. Mrs Cunningham was the picture of good health and good cheer, even though the events of the last few minutes had come close to changing that assessment on both counts.

"I hear you have opted for the religious life, Yvette. Does that rule out mulled wine?"

It was a tradition with the Cunninghams, after a day's winter activities, to gather round the fireplace with a plate of sandwiches and a thermos jug of mulled wine. (With hot chocolate for any youngsters.)

"Goodness, no! I like wine, whether it's mulled or not, thank you, Mrs Cunningham."

"And do you still like Oka cheese?" Mrs Cunningham remembered that smelly Oka, made in a monastery just west of Montreal, had been Yvette's favourite sandwich filling.

"If you can still put up with the smell," laughed Yvette.

"Well then, you'd better get that toboggan back up the hill, and fetch your belongings. The wine will be ready by the time you get your things put away."

# Chapter 2

## Mulled Wine by the Fireplace

The first thing to know about the Cunningham's cottage, is that it is not a cottage. Not in the dictionary sense of being "a small, simple house, typically one in the country". There is no question about its being in the country. On this point the lexicographers were spot on. But small it was not, and by no stretch of the imagination could it be described as simple.

The Cunningham's cottage was, in fact, bigger than their house in Montreal. It could sleep 12 people on beds of some kind, and many more by pressing sofas, mattresses, inflatable rafts and reclining deck chairs into service. It was not unheard of for 20 people to draw up their chairs around the dining table.

The second thing to know, is that 3 generations of Cunninghams had left their marks on the cottage. Some of these marks were in the form of furnishings that were too big, or too worn, or too out-of-fashion, for their city houses. Some were souvenirs from trips to far off places long ago, like the Egyptian tapestries hanging in the cavernous living room. And some were presents from the many guests who had enjoyed the Cunningham's hospitality through the years. All of these things joined forces with the normal paraphernalia of an active family, to give the cottage what an estate agent would probably have described as a "lived-in" look.

The look was more lived-in than ever at this point. The Cunninghams, as usual, had celebrated Christmas at the cottage, and all the decorations were still up. This year no stockings had been "hung by the chimney with care". But two generations of Cunningham children had hung them there, and the nails were still in the mantelpiece, ready for the stockings of the next generation. The mantelpiece itself was strewn with this year's crop of Christmas cards, and on the walls there were Christmas paintings that the children had done when they were in school. There was even a painting that John's father had done when he was in school.

The Christmas tree, whose branches were festooned with colourful decorations, many of which had special meaning to some member of the family, stood in a stand that John in his tenders years had "helped" his father, Duncan Cunningham, to make out of an old tub. It held enough water to keep the tree going for a whole week, if everybody had to go back to Montreal for that long.

He remembered how Grandpa had ridiculed this new-fangled idea of standing the Christmas tree in water. As far as he was concerned, it should be spiked onto a base made from crossed two-by-fours. That's the way he had done it, and that's the way his parents had done it. The fact that this resulted in the branches turning brown and shedding their needles, which needed to be swept up every day, was all part of the Christmas tradition as far as Grandpa was concerned.

However, when he had seen that first tree, still green when the time came to take it down, with a new growth of even brighter green on the ends of many of its branches, he grudgingly conceded that it might be an advantage not to have to sweep up the floor every day. The children had speculated that perhaps the tree might like something to eat, as well as drink, and they had offered it many items of nourishment during the early years—everything from ice cream to Yorkshire pudding, which for some reason Sarah didn't like. Visitors had suggested such disparate things as sugar lumps and aspirin, quoting authorities of impeccable scientific reputation.

When the time had come to throw out that first tree, with its green shoots, John had felt sorry for it. Throwing out a brown tree that was obviously dead was one thing. But this one was still alive! With his father's help, he had thawed the frozen ground with a blow torch, dug a hole and planted the tree, reasoning that if it started to grow again, then they would only have "borrowed" it for Christmas. In fact, they might even be able to borrow it again next Christmas! But he had learned, to his sorrow, that wishful thinking has no impact on the laws of nature.

John put on a stack of well-worn Christmas records Not only did he know all the carols on the records off by heart, having sung many of them himself in both school and church choirs when he was growing up, but he knew all the scratches on the records as well. Yet he never tired of hearing the familiar old songs. They were one of the things that made Christmas Christmas.

Mrs Cunningham had put a plate of sandwiches on the table in front of the fireplace, and was now heading back in that direction with a tray containing small, handled glasses, and a large thermos jug. John put another log on the fire and sat down.

"Well, is this the last time you'll be tasting mulled wine?" Andrew asked Yvette, somewhat awkwardly, as they all clicked their glasses together.

"Don't you remember what happened at Cana?" replied Yvette, whose eyes twinkled the way John remembered they used to when she was enjoying herself.

Yvette knew that Andrew would remember. All the Cunningham children had attended an Anglican Sunday school, where one of the many Bible stories they had listened to was that of the wedding feast in Cana. Although Duncan Cunningham himself had been a Presbyterian when he met Mary Austin, an Anglican, and asked her on bended knee to become Mrs Cunningham, he had decided, as the practical man he was, that it would simplify things to have only one church to attend on Sundays. So he had become an Anglican, and that was that.

"Jesus turned water into wine. Oodles of it," Yvette continued. If he had disapproved of drinking, he would have turned wine into water! Monasteries have been producing wine ever since, and you can be sure that monks and nuns sample the wares before putting them on sale! Dom Pérignon was a Benedictine monk."

"Yvette, dear, tell us about your plans. I understand that you will be entering a convent in the very near future. Is that the final commitment? "

Mrs Cunningham asked this as a mother. Her firm belief was that what was important for young people was to find something that motivated them, something that they could look forward to when they got up in the morning— every morning for the rest of their lives. Money, status and power should never be primary goals in her view. She agreed with Alfred Nobel, who reportedly felt that "contentment is the only real wealth". She wanted to hear Yvette tell her that she had found something that would give her contentment.

"Perhaps you know that since we last met, I have been studying mathematics and classical languages at University. During the past two years I have also been an aspirant at Ste Marie d'en Haut convent, which has involved 'living out', but joining the community at special times for retreats and spiritual preparation. Now that I have obtained my degree, the next step is to become a postulant, which involves living in the convent. I will be embarking on this stage next week."

"So its goodbye, carnal world?"

"There are still a number of steps before the commitment is final. After a year as a postulant, I will become a novice for another year or two, then make temporary vows, which I have to renew annually for a few

years. Only after that, do I take my final vows. At any stage
before my final vows, I can decide not to proceed.
However, if this turns out to be what God wants me to do, it
is likely that we won't meet again outside convent walls."

"So next week you will be leaving the outside world,
for ever and ever, amen?" asked Sarah with a gulp.

"Well, I've seen quite a lot of the outside world in 22
years", replied Yvette with a smile. What I've seen has
convinced me that I can serve God better without its
distractions. But more important, God has asked me to join
his community."

"I'll bet your Mother Superior would have reservations,
if she had seen you commandeering the toboggan!" said
Andrew.

Yvette smiled.

John burst into song.

"No, no! That's wrong!" exclaimed Sarah. "It's *not*
'God rest ye, *merry gentlemen*'"—for that is what John had
just sung, along with the record. "It's '*God rest ye merry,
gentlemen*'". This was a favourite bone of contention in the
Cunningham family at Christmastime. Andrew, for his part
had suggested that the comma should be placed after 'rest',
with the unassailable logic that otherwise 'ye' would be the
object of the verb 'rest', and should therefore be 'you'. They
had asked their mother to adjudicate, but she had
laughingly replied that it didn't matter, as long as everyone
was merry. When they had turned to their father, he had
replied that it didn't matter, as long as everyone sang on
key.

Whilst Sarah and John had been arguing, Andrew had
gone over to the record player and moved the needle back
to the beginning. This time they tried to drown each other
out with their different versions. Not to be left out, Yvette
chimed in—in French.

"Well, I need some help with the dinner," announced Mrs Cunningham. "Sarah and Andrew, you haven't done anything useful all day. You are both volunteered. John and Yvette deserve a rest after their strenuous journey."

The children were used to their mother's good-natured bossing them around. Although they had protested when they were younger, they eventually learned that doing something her way was the fastest way to get it over with. As they grew older, they had come to appreciate her remarkable ability to organize, apparently effortlessly and on the spur of the moment, the most disparate groups of people, to accomplish even seemingly impossible tasks. Preparing dinner was not one of those impossible tasks, but they guessed—correctly—that their mother felt John and Yvette needed some time on their own.

"John, why don't you and Yvette sit down in Granny's annexe? I'm sure you've got a lot to talk about. I turned the heat up just before you arrived"

When Duncan Cunningham's older brother and sister had started their families, their father had helped them to build their own cottages along the lake. By the time it was Duncan's turn, his parents had begun to feel that their cottage was too big for them to look after, even with the Laportes' help. So, with the assistance of their younger son, they had built an annexe for themselves, and handed the main cottage over to him.

This arrangement had the advantage that, when Granny and Grandpa were not there, the annexe could be used as guest accommodation. Now that the grandchildren were all grown up, and Granny and Grandpa no longer felt it was worth risking their antiquated bones on the ski slopes, they had started to spend their winters in Florida.

If God had happened to look down at this instant, he would have seen one of his faithful servants being led off in the direction of the annexe by a non-believer. However, if he was worried, he did not show it in any of the usual ways.

Darkness did not descend over the earth. There were no locusts. Not even a few frogs. Perhaps God had confidence in his servant's ability to handle the situation.

# Chapter 3

## *Theology in the Annexe*

The annexe was a comfortable apartment for two people. On the top level there was a large bedroom, a living room with a kitchenette, and jutting out towards the lake, with a wonderful view on three sides, a "breakfast room". The lower floor, which was only half as big because the house was built on the side of a hill, consisted of a guest bedroom and a game room, which currently held a ping-pong table and an exercise bicycle.

John and Yvette sat down in the living room, in two large wing chairs, which had probably started their careers in the library of John's great-grandparents. Through the windows they could see the lake in all its winter splendour.

"I guess you won't be seeing many views like this from now on," suggested John.

"Are the only views you see, the ones in front of your eyes?"

"I must admit that I have trouble seeing the ones behind me!"

"But what about the ones *inside* you?"

John stopped to think. "Well, when I am dreaming, I see some unusual views. Even when I'm daydreaming, I see the occasional view of merit. However, I wouldn't want to miss out on the real thing."

"But what you are referring to as "the real thing" is only a brief instant in the whole of eternity. I am more interested in the views that are eternal."

"You mean the World to Come, and all that?"

"If, by 'all that', you mean 'the World of Eternal Values', the answer is 'yes'."

"But suppose that the World to Come, doesn't come? Wouldn't it be a shame to have missed out on all those beautiful views?"

"What has happened to your faith since our paths separated? Have you become an atheist?" To John's surprise, Yvette asked this last question with no sign of disapproval, almost as if she were asking him if he had taken up golf.

When John and Yvette had known each other, he had been active in a church youth group, and their Christian faith was another one of the things that had drawn them together. After high-school, he had spent a year hitch-hiking across Asia to Australia, during which time he had encountered a number of other religions. Then, with his wanderlust at least temporarily appeased, he had studied biology at university, where he was now doing post-graduate work. All of this had brought John to the conclusion that there are other possible answers to the big questions, for which he had earlier turned to religion for guidance.

"That depends on what you mean by 'atheist'. If you mean someone who does not believe in the God of the Bible, then I am an atheist. But if you mean someone who discounts the possibility of any form of intelligence outside the world as we know it, then I am not."

John was aware that this was not a statement of belief that would move mountains. Nor was it likely to inspire men—or women—to great deeds. Yvette definitely had the advantage here. She could answer the question "What do you believe in?" with a single, three-letter word. And if the questioner required elaboration, she could refer him to the 18 volumes of *The Catholic Encyclopedia*.

"I mean belief in the Christian God, of course."

"Could you be a bit more specific? Did that God create the world in 6 days and take a rest on the 7th, as described in the Christian Bible?"

John felt that he had made a good point. But Yvette didn't bat an eye. Both of those lovely windows onto her soul, which John had gazed tenderly into so many times in the past, reflected a sense of peace with the world—and slight amusement with what the world had provided for her entertainment this afternoon.

"When you used to tell me that something you were busy with would only take five more minutes, and then not show up for two hours, did you really mean that you would be finished in 300 seconds, or did you mean 'soon'? I would like to think that you don't regard me as being so simple-minded that I would interpret every 2000-year-old Greek or Hebrew phrase in the Bible literally."

"I take your point. But a lot of Christians *do* believe that God created the world in 6 days, just as it is described in Genesis."

"A lot of atheists believe in horoscopes and ouija boards, but I don't hold you accountable for their beliefs. Neither can I, nor the Catholic Church, be held accountable for the beliefs of all Christians."

This was not going to be easy. Ever since John had met Yvette at that dinner party, and learned of her plans to become a nun, he had been rehearsing whatever arguments he could come up with against believing in God. Or at least against the wisdom of devoting one's self so single-mindedly to such a belief that one shut off the outside world—including any members of the opposite sex whose romantic interests may have been reawakened. Yvette had agreed to spend a couple of days at the cottage for old time's sake, on the strict condition that John behave "as a gentleman".

John interpreted this as a measure of physical separation, with "arm's length" being a reasonably gentlemanly distance, and agreed readily to the condition. His hope was to win back Yvette's heart, not to conquer her body, despite the undoubted attractions of the latter.

In fact, the task was harder than that, for John was not completely sure that he *did* want to win back Yvette's affection. He certainly did not want to end up in a position where he had to break off their relationship for a second time. Yvette was a different person from the girl he used to know. A lot happens in the next five years, when you're 17 years old. During that period, and until today, John had only met Yvette once, at the dinner party. Suppose he did succeed in getting her to abandon her current plans, and later decided that she wasn't the person he wanted to spend the rest of his life with after all. He would have taken away from her something that has obviously given her a sense of purpose in life, and could possibly make her deliriously happy, and replaced it with—what?

"You answered my second question, but not my first one," continued Yvette. "What caused you to loose your faith?"

This wasn't at all the way John had envisaged it. *He* was supposed to be doing the cross-examining. But at least Yvette was showing an interest in him.

"There was no single event. Little bits got chipped off the God I believed in from time to time, until one morning I woke up and realized that there was nothing left. However, I can identify the moment when I felt the first twinge of discomfort with my belief."

"When was that?"

"It was shortly after we split up. One of the ministers in our church had preached a sermon at a service attended by our youth group, and we sat around afterwards drinking coffee with him. I asked him about one of the Christian dogmas that he had mentioned in his sermon, which I simply didn't understand. It turned out that he didn't understand it either. Or if he did, he certainly couldn't explain it to us. What's more, he made me feel that I had stepped out of line by asking the question—and even more so by not accepting his answer."

"What was the dogma?"

"His sermon had touched upon the so-called Vicarious Atonement, the notion that Jesus' death on a cross 2000 years ago somehow gets me off the hook for the sins I commit today."

Laughing suited Yvette. She did it spontaneously and without a trace of malice. Her whole body seemed to take part. Her lips parted to reveal an expanse of white teeth, which did credit to the skill of her dentist, who had removed the last braces shortly after John met her on the ski slopes. But above all, she laughed with her eyes. They conveyed her delight even without the rest of the fireworks.

Yvette laughed now. "I can understand why the minister was disconcerted. You went straight for the jugular! You challenged a doctrine that is central to the Christian faith. If Christ had not died for our redemption, then his death would have been in vain, and the Christian Church would be built on sand."

"But I didn't challenge anything. I asked him to explain it."

"What was his explanation?"

"He mumbled something about its being the "Great Mystery of Redemption"— how God took to himself the nature of man, and being both God and Man, became the mediator between God and men."

"That sounds like part of a very orthodox explanation. What was your objection?"

"I already *knew* it was a great mystery! What I wanted was an *explanation* of the mystery, not to be told that it was one. And as far as I was concerned, his reference to Jesus being both God and Man—and for that matter also the Son of God and the Son of Man—simply referred this unsolved mystery to another one, that of the Trinity."

"What is it that you find difficult to understand about the doctrine of Atonement?"

"To me it makes as much sense as if we were to grab some poor man off the street, string him up, and then say 'OK. He has been executed for all the crimes which people will commit in the future. So we have no further use of our justice system.'"

"But God didn't grab Jesus off the street. Mankind had sinned against God's commandments, and for that the punishment was death. But God's love was so great that he came down to earth, took human form and died willingly in our place. Jesus *chose* to die for us."

"So if a father turns up at a police station and says 'Arrest me and punish me for all the crimes which my children and their children may commit in the future', that would be OK?"

"No. You have overlooked something of fundamental importance."

"What is that?"

"Only the person who is sinned against can forgive the sinner. If that father had gone to the police station and said 'Arrest me and punish me for all the crimes which anyone may commit *against me* in the future. I forgive every one of them, who truly repents and asks for forgiveness,' then you would have had a much better analogy."

It was all John could do to stop himself from applauding. This was a brilliant reply. Once again he became aware that life with Yvette would be nothing if not intellectually stimulating. This did not mean that her reply had brought him any closer to believing in God. As far as John was concerned, Yvette had also overlooked something of fundamental importance, namely, the possibility that there was no God. If the God of the Bible existed only in the minds of men, then he could not be sinned against, he could not forgive anyone, and above all—he could not transform himself into a human being and let himself be crucified. This was a big "if".

However, John didn't want to break the magic of the moment by bringing up this show-stopper. He was once again enjoying her company, and wanted to get to know the new Yvette better.

"That was a much better answer than the minister gave me! But do you mean that once Jesus had been confirmed dead, it became open season for anyone to commit any sin he pleased, since God had promised him forgiveness beforehand?"

"He would have to truly repent of his sins and pray for forgiveness."

"So if Hitler in his bunker in 1945 had said he was sorry for all the innocent people he had gassed to death, and asked for forgiveness, God would have forgiven him?"

"I cannot speak for God, of course, but my understanding is that if Hitler had genuinely repented and prayed for forgiveness with all his heart, then God would have forgiven him. However, this doesn't necessarily mean that he would have escaped punishment. He would not have been found innocent of his crimes."

"In Scotland, instead of finding a person 'guilty' or 'innocent', a court can hand down a 'not-proven' verdict. It would appear that in God's court there is a fourth possibility: 'guilty but forgiven'!"

"God is not interested in legalese. God cares about what's in your heart. And right now I suspect that God is saddened to see that your heart is no longer filled with love for Him. But He still loves you, and longs to welcome you back into His family."

Once again, John refrained from pointing out that if there was no God, he could neither love anyone nor conduct any welcoming ceremonies. He realized, however, that the subject could not be put off indefinitely.

"Has it ever occurred to you, to question the existence of God?"

"Has it ever occurred to you, to question my existence?"

"No. But I can see you. I can hear you. I can touch you." At this, John stretched out his hand and placed it gently on Yvette's, which was resting on the arm of her chair.

The world stopped for a few seconds. John felt Yvette's hand start to turn, as if to grasp his. Then it went limp again. He guessed that this had been a reflex reaction, which had been nipped in the bud once her cerebral cortex had kicked in. He removed his hand.

"I can hear God," replied Yvette. "And he can hear me. We converse every day."

One of the many relics in the Cunningham's cottage was a bookcase containing an old leather-bound edition of the *Encyclopedia Britannica,* which had once resided in the library of John's grandparents, and whose pages were embellished with pencilled-in comments made by his father during his formative years. John had consulted this venerable work frequently in preparation for Yvette's visit.

He was convinced that the authors of the article "God, arguments for the existence of" had done their best. Their explanations of the Ontological, Cosmological, Teleological and other arguments were paragons of clarity, and John had almost committed them to memory. But the authors had concentrated their efforts on the conventional weapons of Christian apologetics. They had left out the atom bomb of arguments: Personal Acquaintance.

How can you argue against the existence of a God that someone has shaken hands with?

"Excuse me for intruding on you love birds, but Mother says that dinner will be ready in ten minutes."

Yvette looked genuinely shocked as she turned to face the messenger. "Sarah! We have been talking about the love of God. There has been no question of any other kind of love."

"Sorry!" said Sarah good-naturedly, "But wasn't there even a touch of human love? Jesus did, after all, tell his disciples to love one another as he had loved them."

It would be a gross exaggeration to say that Yvette's cheeks took on the colour of ripe tomatoes. They did not. But there was enough of a hint of that hue to suggest that she might have been guilty of letting her thoughts dwell, however briefly, on a form of love that had neither God nor disciples as protagonists.

# Chapter 4

## A Second Christmas Dinner

Sarah and Andrew had not been twiddling their thumbs whilst the theological discussion was going on next door. They had set the table with all the finery of Christmas. There was the hand-woven runner, running the length of the table, which had been in the family for so long that no one was sure where it had come from. It was embroidered with elves and Yule logs. As a child, John had thought it looked so old that it must predate Christianity. On top of the runner were poinsettias, candelabras, and bowls of fruit, figs, dates and nuts. On individual red place mats, there were china plates, crystal glasses and silver cutlery—all family heirlooms—and linen napkins that had been folded to resemble fleurs-de-lis, the emblem of Quebec.

"Is the Queen coming for dinner, Mrs Cunningham?" asked Yvette in wonder.

"Not the Queen," replied her hostess with a friendly smile, "But a very special guest whom we haven't seen for many years. So we have decided to have a second Christmas dinner in her honour. The turkey isn't as big this time, but it's big enough for the five of us, and there will be enough left over to make turkey sandwiches for lunch and Turkey à la King for dinner some evening."

"Five of us. Isn't Mr Cunningham coming?"

"No. He has decided to stay in Montreal for another day or two."

If Duncan Cunningham felt that the business empire, which three generations of Cunningham's had built up, required his presence at the helm during this Christmas season, no one present was about to question his judgement. They were aware that he was the one who made it all possible. Although this titan of the business world, who was an unpretentious man, would have recoiled at the thought, it was as if an invisible hand had discretely placed an embossed card with the message "Courtesy of Duncan Cunningham, Esq." on the table that had been prepared for this mid-winter feast.

"John, I've put you on this side with Sarah, so that you can help me carry things in. Yvette, you're on the other side beside Andrew."

With almost military precision, Mrs Cunningham brought in the turkey, followed by her foot soldiers carrying plates of roasted potatoes, squash, peas and a boat full of gravy.

She gave the signal to sit down and five chairs scraped in unison. Five mouths also watered in unison at the sight and aroma of this repast.

"Would you like white meat, dark, or some of both Yvette?"

"A bit of both, please, Mrs Cunningham."

John couldn't help smiling as he remembered a Christmas many years ago, when it had been their turn to host Christmas dinner for the Cunningham clan. Andrew, who might have been about six at the time, was sitting at the "children's table", too far away to see that his father was carving a turkey. So when he was asked what kind of meat he wanted, Andrew, who was fond of roast beef, replied "red meat, please".

After everyone had been served, Mrs Cunningham raised her glass and said "Bon appetite!" knowing full well that it was unnecessary to wish a good appetite on four people, whose appetites could not be improved upon. But this was the agreed-upon starting signal, and no one needed any further encouragement.

"I hope John hasn't been harassing you with his agnostic nonsense, Yvette, dear. I don't know where he gets it all."

It was a source of sorrow to Mary Cunningham that her eldest son seemed to have lost his faith in God. Although she did not make a show of her religion, she felt that it was what knit society together and gave it its backbone. However, she was too wise to argue with him. She hoped that it was just another phase he was going through.

"He did express some sceptical thoughts, all right. But I didn't feel in the least harassed. If we never question our faith, then it's not really our own. We have just accepted somebody else's faith, lock stock and barrel."

"Good for you, Yvette! I thought you would be able to handle him. Perhaps you can talk some sense into him."

"Faith is something that has to come from within, Mrs Cunningham. I can't make John believe any more than I can make the proverbial horse drink water. John has already drunk from the trough of religion, and he seems to have spat it out."

There is a wide-spread convention in polite society that politics and religion should be avoided as topics of dinner-table conversation. The Cunninghams were, on the whole, as polite as any family—indeed, more so than many. However, succeeding generations of Cunningham parents had taken the stance that it was at the dinner table they had the best chance of encouraging their children to discuss things intelligently and with respect for others. So within the family—and Yvette was almost family—no topics were barred. Only impoliteness, disrespect—and dullness.

"Well, I don't know what kind of society he thinks we would have if people stopped believing in God. What would keep people from running around shooting each other?"

This was an example of what Mary Cunningham's husband laughingly called her "Tea-and-cake proof" of God's existence. (According to him) his wife felt God's presence most strongly in a room full of god-fearing people who had come together to do good works—and enjoy each other's home baking. God made people good; therefore he existed.

"There were apparently a lot of god-fearing people shooting one another during the American Civil War," suggested Andrew. Religion wasn't a topic that Andrew spent a lot of time thinking about. He seemed to have inherited his father's pragmatism. If religion helped to hold society together, and prevented people from doing evil, then he was all for it. He was happy to leave the theology to theologians. This contribution was probably made more to add spice to the conversation than through any desire to challenge his mother's beliefs.

"But they didn't shoot at one another *because* of their religion," objected Sarah, who probably held the most orthodox religious views in the family. "That war was fought over slavery. Sometimes good people have to take up arms to combat evil. Where would we be today if Christian men had not taken up arms against Hitler?"

"It wasn't only Christian men who fought—and laid down their lives—in the Second World War," John pointed out. "But what I would like to know is: why does God let men do things like that to each other? If God is sitting up there watching our every move, listening to our every prayer, and all the while loving us, as the Bible tells us he does, why doesn't he stop us from killing one another?"

"He has told us what to do in the Bible, and Jesus has shown us how to do it. But we choose to ignore Him. It's just like an earthly father. He can teach his children how to behave. But he can't live their lives for them. Once they are grown up, if they choose to rebel against what he has taught them, he can only look on in sorrow." Yvette sounded almost as if she were teaching a class of Sunday school children.

Once again, John realized that Yvette was begging the question of God's existence. *If* God exists, and *if* the Bible is the word of God, and *if* Jesus is the son of God, then Yvette's reasoning had a lot going for it. Otherwise, the Bible is as relevant as any other collection of human writings. But John wasn't about to go straight for the jugular, as Yvette had so picturesquely put it. Instead he tried a gentler approach.

"Are we 'grown up' in the eyes of God? Has he decided that there is nothing more he can do except look on in sorrow?"

"He has given us a free will," replied Yvette matter-of-factly. "If he intervened, he would be violating our free will."

"Then what about prayer?" asked John. "If there is no chance of God's intervention, doesn't that make prayer a waste of time?"

"Oh, but John, don't you see? That's different! God *can* intervene if we *ask* him to. It's just that God can't intervene without being asked." Sarah's faith was uncomplicated. "Jesus loves me, this I know; for the Bible tells me so" summarized the salient points of her theology.

"There must be something more required, than just a request for intervention. Think of all the mothers who have watched their children slowly dying of cancer. Don't you suppose some of them have asked God to intervene?"

"The problem with you, John," said his mother, "is that you expect to be able to understand everything. Some things have to be taken on faith. Look at Ron. When we tell him to get into the car, he doesn't know why, or where we are going to take him. He doesn't understand how a car works. But he trusts us to do what is best for him."

"Ah, but there is a big difference," exclaimed John. "Ron can see us. He can feel us. He has watched us put food into his bowl. He has good reason to have faith in us. In contrast, the Bible asks us to believe in a God whom *no one* has ever seen or interacted with in any verifiable way."

"Maybe we're just not equipped to see Him," suggested Andrew. "Humans aren't that far removed from dogs. I suspect good old Ron has a pretty good idea what's going on in our minds a lot of the time. But consider a bacterium in my gut. It has no way of knowing anything about me, or understanding where the bits of turkey that float past it have come from—even though the evidence is all around it. The difference between a lowly human being and someone capable of creating the universe must be at least as great as that between a bacterium and me."

"I'll grant you, there is nothing to say that there could not be some form—or forms—of intelligence all around us, which we are too unintelligent to comprehend. But that does not make the God of the Bible any more likely. The Bible doesn't claim that God is a being whose attributes we can't comprehend. On the contrary, it states that God has created us humans "in his own image", which—if it means anything—must mean that God has endowed us with some of his own attributes.

"The Bible goes on to say that God loves us, approves of certain behaviour and disapproves of other, intervenes occasionally to heal the sick and raise the dead, has turned himself into a human male, who ascended physically into something called heaven after having been crucified, and who—according to the theologians, at least—turns bread and wine into flesh and blood respectively, whenever certain incantations have been recited."

"Oh, John. You're so callous!" exclaimed Sarah.

"It does all sound a bit devoid of love and compassion," concurred Yvette, whose demeanour gave no reason to suspect a lack of either of these qualities.

The damnedest thing is—she's right! thought John to himself. It was just as his mother had always said: belief in God gives people a sense of being part of something bigger than themselves and gives them a reason to love and help their fellow men. John was acutely aware that his lack of belief had very little to offer by way of alternative. "Onward Faithless Soldiers" just didn't have the same rousing appeal as its Christian counterpart. This was why he was reluctant to pull out all the stops.

Suppose his arguments were to shatter the rock-solid faith that gave Yvette her serene tranquillity. If he could offer her something in its place—for example the opportunity of becoming Mrs John Cunningham—it would be one thing. But he was not prepared to take that step. At any rate not yet.

Despite having just been accused of callousness and lack of love and compassion, he was not so devoid of those last two qualities that he would not suffer pangs of remorse, if he felt that he had holed the boat of certainty that was carrying Yvette over the turbulent sea of life, and left her to flounder without a life belt.

"Maybe God has put those thoughts into your mind," suggested Sarah, "to discourage us from trying to find a logical reason for believing in Him. Faith has to be just that: faith; a 'leap in the dark'. God is outside the jurisdiction of science and logic."

"If he's doing that," replied John, trying hard not to sound triumphant, "then he has violated my free will. I have certainly not invited him to put those, or any other, thoughts into my head!"

Andrew came to Sarah's rescue. "Sarah's right, you know. There can never be any logically compelling reason for believing in God. If there were, someone would have found it long ago, and everyone in the world would be a believer."

"By the same token," added Yvette, with apparently faultless logic, "if there were any logically compelling reason for *not* believing in God, someone would have found *that* long ago, and *no one* in the world would be a believer."

"I don't agree with either of you," said John. "It's like saying that there is no logically compelling reason for believing—or not believing—in Gazonks. What is a Gazonk? If a Gazonk can be anything you want it to be, and change its nature at will, then trying to find reasons for believing in it or not is a futile exercise. But once a Gazonk—or God—is said to interact with our world in a specific way, this can be investigated, and may even be possible to prove or disprove. For example, it is possible to disprove that the loud noise associated with lightning is caused by the god Thor hammering on his anvil."

To keep our minds focused on the main thread of conversation during this meal, the chronicler has withheld dialogue relating to a secondary thread. Some indication of how it developed can be gleaned from the following snippets. "This is delicious!" "Would you pass the gravy please?" "Is the cranberry sauce home made?" "Would you like some more?" "If I have another little piece of turkey, am I allowed to have a big spoonful of that wonderful stuffing?"

This theme became the dominant one as the time approached for dessert. Plates were brought out to the kitchen, clean plates were placed on the table, lamps were turned off, leaving only candles to light the room, and Mary Cunningham arrived from the kitchen bearing the *pièce de résistance*—the plum pudding, *en flambé*.

When the applause had died down, she said "I've made both kinds of sauce, Yvette. I remember that you used to like hard sauce."

Every family has its special traditions at Christmastime. In Mary Austin's family, the plum pudding had always been served with (cold) hard sauce, whereas in Duncan Cunningham's, it was served with (hot) brandy sauce. Since her husband had, on his own initiative, converted to her religion, Mary (by now Cunningham) felt that the least she could do by way of reciprocation was to learn to make her mother-in-law's brandy sauce. In this she had succeeded so well, that many cookbooks in the Eastern Townships today contained hand-written insertions entitled "Mary Cunningham's Brandy Sauce", although the attribution should, of course, have been to Frances Cunningham, Duncan's mother. Each Christmas in the Cunningham household, the relative merits of hard vs brandy sauce were debated every bit as vigorously as the correct position for the comma in "God Rest(,) Ye(,) Merry(,) Gentlemen".

"Thank you, Mrs Cunningham. Your brandy sauce is delicious, too. But it is not unlike some French sauces, whereas I've never run into hard sauce anywhere else."

John remembered how, many Christmases ago, his mother had inadvertently left him alone for a few moments within reach of a plate of hard sauce and a spoon. Until that fateful day, he had liked his sauce hard. Ever since, he had been much more open-minded. The ensuing discomfort of that evening had, years later, led to John's wondering if it might have been a similar experience that lay behind Shakespeare's conclusion that, where sweetness is concerned, "a little more than a little is by much too much". The feeling of kinship which this had engendered with the Bard, had made studying his assigned works during John's school years less burdensome than many of his classmates had found it to be.

For readers unfamiliar with the culinary traditions associated with an English Christmas, it should be mentioned that brandy sauce, as its name implies, contains a generous quantity of that spirit. Hard sauce contains an equally generous quantity of rum (although much smaller

quantities of these spirits had been used by Mrs
Cunningham when the children were small). It should also
be pointed out that during this meal more than one bottle of
a certain sparkling wine had been consumed. According to
Mr Cunningham, from whose cellar it came, it was German
Champagne. The rest of his family suspected that he
deliberately called it thus in order to upset the "wine snobs"
(his term), who insisted that it was *sekt.*

The aforementioned stimulants joined forces with the
natural high spirits of the Cunningham family to produce a
Christmas atmosphere, which in every respect was worthy
of the epithet *merry.*

"John, you got off easy this afternoon, so you can do
the washing up. Andrew and Yvette can dry. Sarah can put
the dishes away, and I'll look after the left-overs."

As the last gurgles from the kitchen sink announced
that another notch could be made on the broomstick, or
wherever it was that Mary Cunningham recorded her
triumphs of household management, she said, "Yvette, why
don't you play something for us?"

Yvette was an accomplished amateur pianist, and had
often added to the conviviality of the Cunningham
household with her playing, both at the cottage and in
Montreal. The cottage piano was a black Heintzman of
ancient vintage, which John and his siblings had all
struggled with when they were taking piano lessons. It had
been moved to the cottage from Montreal when Mary
Cunningham had inherited a mahogany Chickering from
her parents.

Yvette stroked the ivory keys, which had not felt the
touch of her fingers for five years, as if they were old
friends. Then, as John would recall later, all hell broke
loose. "Rockin' Around the Christmas Tree", a current hit
on the pop charts, was not a tune that you could listen to
with intellectual detachment. Nor did anyone in the present
company attempt to do so. Even Mary Cunningham's

somewhat matronly figure took on a more youthful aspect, as it swayed in time with the music, and everyone joined in with the lyrics.

It is said that Great Uncle Alasdair Cunningham, a Presbyterian man of the cloth (RIP), left his parishioners in no doubt as to what was encompassed by the term "joyful noise" in Psalm 100. We need be in no doubt that the singing which, if not actually lifting the rafters of that snow-bound cottage, certainly shook off the dust, would not have qualified.

As John watched Yvette's ponytail swinging back and forth, it was difficult for him to picture her in a nun's habit. Didn't they have to shave their heads? At any rate, he doubted whether pony-tails would be allowed. And even if they were—what would be the point? There would be no male hearts to beat faster at the sight of them. In fact, there would be no sight of them at all beneath all that black cloth!

"That was wonderful, Yvette!" said Mary Cunningham, whose soprano voice, although more accustomed to the standard repertoire of church choirs, had held its own against those of her offspring. "But would your Mother Superior have approved?"

"Why should the Devil have all the good music?" asked Yvette, with that mischievous glint in her eye that reawakened long-slumbering emotions in John's bosom— and made him realize that perhaps he was going to have to take that step.

Without stopping to acknowledge the applause, Yvette started in on "God rest ye merry gentlemen", leaving it up to the Cunninghams to insert commas where they saw fit.

It is said that all good things must come to an end. The chronicler suspects that, as was the case with all swans being white, a single counter-example—of some wonderful thing showing no sign of ever being brought to a conclusion—may some day be found, which would call into question the validity of that aphorism. However, the events of this evening did not provide such a refutation. After half a dozen or so well-loved carols had been sung with great gusto, minds began to wander. Concentration was no longer what it had been during the first refrain of "Rockin' Around".

And Ron let it be known that he had been neglected long enough.

"Who's going to take Ron out for his walk?" asked Mrs Cunningham.

John had often reflected on why dogs needed to be taken for walks in the country. All you need to do is open the door, and the dog can go out for a walk on its own. Or a run, if it prefers. He often suspected that it was the humans who needed the walk. Tonight he could think of two humans who might benefit from a walk together.

"I would enjoy the walk," replied Yvette, whose quick response ensured her a position at the head of the queue.

John hoped that Yvette's alacrity was an indication that she shared his opinion regarding the potential benefits of a walk together in the cold night air.

"May I join you?" asked John.

"Avec plaisir."

# Chapter 5

## A Walk Under the Stars

If you, dear reader, have lived your life in a city, you may never have gazed at a night sky such as that which extended its dome over the threesome slowly making its way along the snow-covered road skirting the shore of Lake Gomareph. From a city street in the northern hemisphere it is sometimes possible, on a winter's night, to see the major stars in Orion, Ursa Major and, if you've got keen eyesight, some of those in Ursa Minor. But, from a country road on a moonless night, with no street lamp in sight, it is possible to see hundreds—nay, thousands—of stars. And they sparkle like diamonds in a coal-black sky—quite unlike the dull light seeping through holes in a moth-eaten curtain, which is what the city dweller sees.

For a few minutes, Yvette and her companion walked on in silence, save for the crunching of snow under their feet, and the sound of Ron galumphing towards the trees, upon which it was his wont to leave his calling card. It didn't matter how many times they had seen it before; they were awestruck by the magnificence of the spectacle above them.

For Yvette, this was another example of God's majesty. For John, things were not so simple. He was acutely aware that if all the atheists in the world from the beginning of time were to combine their best efforts, they would never be able to come up with anything on this scale. Whether we choose to call it God, or give it a different name, we all look to something bigger than ourselves for an explanation.

The Big Bang Theory—ironically, proposed by a Roman Catholic priest—suggests that the whole universe had at some point in time been concentrated into a single "primeval atom", or "cosmic egg", which exploded and has been expanding ever since.

But does this help? The fact that all matter has been (much) closer together at some point in time doesn't answer the question as to where it came from in the first place. Nor does saying that it all started out as energy bring us any closer to an ultimate explanation. Where did the energy come from?

The alternative theory that has been put forward to provide a scientific explanation for the origin of the universe, the Steady State Theory, basically says "It has always been there". This comes no closer to providing a first cause.

There's no question about it: the God Theory provides the simplest answer. It is the ultimate Theory of Everything: God is omnipotent, therefore he can create whatever he pleases, and there's an end to it. It's not necessary for us to understand the finer points of how he goes about it.

However, John felt that this was not a theory upon which a successful modern society could be based, even if it probably served its purpose for desert tribes in an earlier millennium. The fact that there are questions we cannot answer, does not mean that God is the answer.

Andrew seemed to have arrived at a pragmatic *modus vivendi*: let God be in charge of the unexplainable things. That frees our minds to concentrate on the things that we *can* explain. What does it matter if God's area of responsibility diminishes over time? In the meantime, he gives us peace of mind and promotes good will amongst men. This approach appealed to John. It meant that we had Christian morals as a starting point, from which we could hopefully develop a more robust moral code, devoid of reliance on supernatural intervention. The question was how long such an evolution would take, and whether other religions would sit around patiently, waiting for our new society to slowly emerge.

"This afternoon you said that Atonement was one of the Christian dogmas that you had trouble with. What are the others?"

Was Yvette hoping to reclaim John for the Christian faith, at the same time that he was trying to wean her off that faith—if, indeed, that is what he was trying to do?

If only everything didn't have to be decided within the next two days! Either he would have to propose to Yvette during this short time together, or else he had no right to interfere in her life. Once she entered the convent, she might never encounter another doubter as long as she lived, and might be supremely happy for the rest of her days.

John did not feel ready to make a life-long commitment. But was he prepared to see Yvette disappear from his life for ever? It was going to be a tumultuous couple of days.

"The virgin birth and the dual nature of Christ were the most intractable ones."

"Don't you suppose that if God is capable of creating the whole world, he might be capable of implanting a foetus in a woman's womb?"

"That's not really the sticking point. It's a question of *what* God implanted in Mary's womb. According to the official dogma, Jesus was both human and divine at the same time."

"You don't think that would be a simple matter for God, after creating the universe?"

"Would it be a simple matter for God to create a stone that was too heavy for him to lift?"

"God is not in the business of creating self-contradictory follies—such as square circles or stones too heavy for him to lift—for the amusement of human philosophers." Formal logic had been part of Yvette's mathematics course at St. Francis Xavier University, and she was not about to be stumped by this old conundrum. "But I don't see the connection."

"If we are to believe Christian dogma, that's exactly what God did create. Jesus is a prime example of what you've just called a 'self-contradictory folly'."

It was difficult for John to see Yvette's reaction. They were both bundled up against the cold and there was no moon. But he didn't need to see it. He could feel it. Her silence was silver-tongued. Had he had done what he had been trying to avoid—gone for the jugular? A person, who has decided to dedicate the rest of her life to her Prince of Glory, cannot be expected to feel joy at hearing that same Prince described as a 'self-contradictory folly'. Should he apologize and start talking about the weather instead?

This is not the course that John chose. Had he thought rationally about it, he would have realized that this must mean something inside him was pushing him towards that long-term commitment. But he didn't think rationally about it. "*Le coeur a ses raisons que la raison ne connaît point*," as Pascal so eloquently put it.

"I hope you noticed the conditional clause: '*if* we are to believe Christian dogma'. Jesus himself cannot be held responsible for the dogma which two millennia of Christian theologians, starting with St Paul, have tacked on to his name. As far as I can make out, Jesus' main message was that we should love one another, and that is neither self-contradictory nor folly."

John wiped his brow with an imaginary handkerchief.

"One part of the dogma," John went on, "asserts that Jesus was 100% human—otherwise we cannot be blamed for failing to live up to his example—whilst another part asserts that Jesus was part of the Trinity, which is 100% God. Is that not a contradictory folly?"

"Do you remember what your mother said about Ron? Some things have to be taken on faith."

"My objection still stands. Ron has personal experience of us. He has learned that he can rely on us. I have no personal experience of God."

"I do," said Yvette quietly. "I experience Him every day. Are you sure that you haven't experienced God? What is making you treat me with so much consideration right now? Why don't you just tell me that everything I believe in would fall apart if God doesn't exist, and be done with it? Something is holding you back, making you try not to hurt my feelings."

All that effort, and all in vain! Yvette had seen through him from the outset. However, it all comes back to that big 'if'. *If* God exists, then, yes, it could be God who has made him want to avoid hurting Yvette at all costs. But that's certainly not the way it felt to John.

"I'm not convinced that God has been motivating me in this matter. It would seem to be a strange way for him to go about it. Why would he first fill me with doubt, and then tell me to tread softly? Why not just fill me with joyous belief and avoid all this hassle?"

"I have no answer," replied Yvette, simply. "I do not know the mind of God. But I shall ask Him for guidance on this issue."

"Whilst you've got his attention, you might ask him about Jesus' DNA."

"What do you mean?" asked Yvette, perplexed.

"Well, if Jesus was 100% human, he must have had 23 pairs of chromosomes like the rest of us. Normally, one member of each pair would come from his mother, and the other from his father. So either God magicked up 23 chromosomes and paired them with 23 from Mary, or else he implanted a complete embryo in her womb." As a biologist, John could not help thinking about this whenever he contemplated the virgin birth.

"Why would creating a few chromosomes be a problem for God?"

"It's a question of the nature of those chromosomes. The Bible tells us that God knew beforehand that Jesus would fulfil the Biblical prophesies about a Messiah, which necessarily required him to live a sinless life."

"So?"

"As you reminded us earlier this evening, God has given us a free will. So, if Jesus was 100% human, he had a free will, and he could have used that free will to reject God altogether, instead of leading a godly life. In the history of the world, as far as we know, no other human, following his own free will, has managed to lead a faultless life. At any rate, not according to the Bible, which says we are all sinners in need of forgiveness. Even the Lord's Prayer assumes that we need forgiveness for our sins.

"So you think it strange that Jesus was able to lead a faultless life when no one else manages to do so?"

"More than strange. It's inexplicable—if we are to believe that he was 100% human. Remember, God told Mary *ahead of time* that her son would be the Son of God and that his kingdom would have no end. So either God was pulling the strings throughout Jesus' career, in which case he was not a normal human being, but a puppet—and therefore irrelevant as a role model for us—or else the genes contained in the chromosomes that God implanted in Mary were such that Jesus had no choice but to be perfect."

"Perhaps that's what God did, then."

"But in that case, you can't claim that Jesus had a free will. He was only free to choose the things that God had decided ahead of time he should do. And if God is able to select genes which can cause *one* person to lead a faultless life, why doesn't he do it for all of us? Think of all the unnecessary human suffering that would be avoided!"

"I can't tell you why God does what he does, or how he does it. In this case, I'm like Ron. I have faith, because God has never failed me. Perhaps if you asked God, he might answer some of your questions."

"Don't you suppose that's already been tried? If all the books that have been written on these 'mysteries of faith' were stacked on top of one another, they would make the Eiffel Tower look like something seen through the wrong end of a telescope. Since most of the books have been written by devout Christians, we can safely assume that the authors have asked God for guidance.

"If any one of those books had come up with an answer, every Bible printed in the world today would include it as an appendix, no further books would be needed on the subject, and the whole of mankind would be united in a common, rock-solid faith. But this has not happened. There is no sign of a slump in the market for books offering explanations of Christian dogma, and hardly a day goes by without some new denomination popping up whose founder has decided that The *True* Truth differs on some point from all the other Truths on offer."

Yvette would doubtless have replied that this does not apply to the Roman Catholic Church, whose doctrine has remained essentially unchanged for centuries, and perhaps have referred John to *The Catholic Encyclopedia* (18 vols) by way of confirmation.

However, she was prevented from doing so by a more urgent matter. On a dark country road, the headlamps of oncoming vehicles can be seen in the sky for a considerable time before the vehicle itself bursts on the scene. Such a glow in the firmament had been the signal for John to put Ron on his leash and for the three of them to move into the deep snow by the side of the road.

It is easy to forget, in haste, that just as the flat surface of a lake reveals nothing about the unevenness of its bottom, neither does new-fallen snow offer any clues as to what unsuitable objects for human feet to be placed on, may be lurking below. This was brought quite suddenly to John's attention when he became aware of the fact that Yvette was embracing him. It was not the gentle embrace of two old friends meeting after an absence. It was more like the passionate embraces that he and Yvette had shared when their relationship had been at its zenith. His arms automatically reciprocated.

As the car broke in on the scene, its headlamps picked out two lovebirds at the side of the road, engaged in a tight embrace. And this is what Mrs Moffat—for it was she who had interrupted their ambulatory theology seminar—reported to a surprised Mrs Cunningham the following morning.

When Yvette had regained her footing, she extricated herself and apologized embarrassedly. John laughed that he was only too happy to have been able to provide support. But inwardly he was not laughing. Yvette's unexpected closeness had affected him. Physically, emotionally, and in every other way that a red-blooded male could be affected. He debated whether to suggest taking a "shortcut" home, on the off chance that further mishaps might bring them into close proximity again. But he decided that would not fall within the bounds of "gentlemanly behaviour", to which was committed.

# Chapter 6

## *Morning in the Cottage*

Steam locomotives had always held a special place in John's heart. They were not smelly, noisy things, like diesel engines, nor were they dull and well-behaved, like electric ones. They had personality. They were swashbuckling. The mere sight of one conjured up visions of adventure and romance.

But this particular steam locomotive conjured up entirely different visions. It was approaching at high speed and John couldn't get out of the way. He seemed to be stuck to the tracks. The driver blew his whistle in warning. Then he leaned out of the window and spoke to him.

"Good morning!"

John managed to prod a few grey cells into action, just enough to send an "open" instruction to his right eyelid. What that eye saw, after a few more instructions had managed to bring things into focus, was an attractive young lady holding a tray on which there appeared to be a mug of tea and some biscuits.

"Your mother thought it was time for you to wake up" said this apparition, putting the tray down on the bedside table.

You can hardly expect billions of grey cells to snap into action, only seconds after being awoken. They would be tripping all over one another in the mad rush. As Yvette, for she it turned out to be, leaned over—which brought her hair, fragrant from recent washing, within inches of John's nostrils—this gentleman forgot his vow. He stretched out his hand and took Yvette's in his.

Yvette did not withdraw her hand. But there was no response. No encouraging squeeze. He might as well have been holding the belt, which dangled lifeless from the knot on her dressing gown.

John's brain cells had taken advantage of this short interlude to rub the sleep from their eyes, and they were now queuing up for the lavatory. Those that had already completed their morning ablutions were starting to come to John's assistance.

The first thing they did was remind him of his promise. But the cells that should have sent out the signal for him to withdraw his hand didn't seem to have reported for duty yet. Instead, a group of early risers pointed out to him that, when you came right down to it, the fair maiden whose hand he was holding had a lot going for her. It wasn't just that she jumped out of bed at the crack of dawn, and could probably be counted on to make the morning tea—although that certainly did not weigh against her. She was also fun to be with, attractive to look at, and—this was the clincher— *he was in love with her.*

It was a bit sneaky of the cells in question to have taken advantage of the early hour to circumvent the MOOT (Ministry Of Orderly Thought). However, John had to admit they were right. He was hooked.

Where did he go from here? Why did *his* grey cells require so much more time to get going in the morning than everyone else's? Just when he needed them most, they were still brushing their teeth.

The only course of action his undermanned brain could come up with was to squeeze Yvette's hand and pull her towards him. If the aforementioned organ had been firing on all cylinders, he would, of course, have been prepared for her reaction. But as it was, he was stymied when she said "John, you promised."

This was uncontroversial. He *had* promised, and he was a man of his word. Besides, it was easy to see that Yvette's short oration could not be interpreted as "You wouldn't respect me if I let you kiss me on our first date." It was a clear case of "Get lost." John released the limp sausage he had been holding.

This put a whole new slant on things. He had been trying to avoid making Yvette fall back in love with him, until he had had a chance to properly assess the pros and cons, draw up a balance sheet, calculate the profit & loss, etc. That she might chose *not* to do so, the moment he let it be known that the position of Mrs J(ohn) L(aughlan) Cunningham might be available, had not entered into his calculations.

John sat up in bed and used his recently liberated hand to pick up the mug of tea. As more of his brain cells turned up for duty, he asked them for an analysis of the situation. The report they came back with was not what he wanted to hear.

Whereas (reports tend to begin in this way) the fair damsel has clearly shown by her use of the so-called "cold-shoulder technique" (CST) that she is not responsive to amorous advances, and

Whereas said damsel has also proved impervious to arguments which might have undermined her religious faith,

Therefore it must be concluded that the damsel in question is hell-bent on becoming a nun, and there is nothing a presumptive suitor can do except watch from the sidelines as she walks through the gates of the convent. And weep.

Those blasted brain cells! Here they had been treated to not one, but two, Christmas dinners, and yet this is the best they could come up with! Defeatists! Bureaucrats! That's what they were. John decided to rebel.

"Yvette."

"Yes?"

"Er ... there's something I'd like to tell you."

"Please do. Why the hesitation? You didn't need any encouragement yesterday," laughed Yvette.

"You're standing too far away."

"I can hear you from here."

"But I can't say what I want to say when you're half way around the world."

Yvette came closer. The mischievous glint was back in her eye. "Are you going to whisper to me that God doesn't exist?"

John picked up the limp sausage again and squeezed it. "No, I'm going to tell you that I will be very sorry to see you walk through those convent gates next week."

Yvette sat down slowly on the edge of the bed. Only a sheet, two blankets and a few nightclothes separated their bodies. "But John, we went through all this five years ago. Back then, I would have been prepared to "love, honour and obey" a mortal for the remainder of my days. But now I have the opportunity to become a bride of Christ."

By this time enough grey cells had clocked in to prevent John from blurting out that Christ would appear to be the ultimate polygamist, with harems of nuns all over the world. Whatever merits such a remark might have had in terms of accuracy, succinctness and wit, it would not have endeared him to a sincere aspirant nun.

"You're not worried that he might not be able to give you his undivided attention?"

"No. God is not subject to human restrictions. He sees and hears not only what we say, but also what we think. And He loves us all, as a parent loves his children— whether we love Him or not."

"But children who are loved by their parents don't usually marry them. They choose people of their own age as partners."

"You should have thought of that five years ago, John. I'm sorry, but in any comparison between you and Jesus, you come in second." Yvette said this with the wistful look of a bride to be. And John was not her intended groom.

The French have a wonderful expression, *esprit d'escalier*, which does not refer to unseen spirits waiting to trip up unsuspecting stair users, but to the witty riposte which arrives after the opportunity to use it has passed, and the slow-witted speaker is on his way downstairs. It was on his way down for breakfast, that John realized he could have offered to take on Jesus in a kissing contest. Then Yvette would have seen who came in second!

Breakfast was a completely informal affair in the Cunningham household. It consisted of whatever you made for yourself. There was no service laid on. It was consumed at the "breakfast table" (which became the luncheon table and the bedtime-snack table, as these needs arose), situated by the kitchen window. From this table there was an unimpeded view of the frozen, snow-covered lake, on which children could be seen building an igloo; anoraks with fur-rimmed hoods, fishing through holes in the ice; cross-country skiers, crossing country; and the occasional deer, wondering where his bathtub had gone.

If perchance there should be, amongst readers of this saga, a sociology student searching for a suitable subject of research, he or she might consider The Enigma of the Human Breakfast. Other meals aim at having as much menu variation as possible from day to day. At any given meal, however, there is no menu variation at all. Everyone gets the same thing for dinner, for example. Exactly the opposite is true of breakfast. Any given person tends to eat the same thing for breakfast every day. There is no menu variation at all from day to day. But at any given breakfast, the menu variation is enormous. Everyone tends to have something different.

On his way downstairs, John had established, from the smells reaching his nostrils, that coffee, toast with cinnamon, orange juice, lemon—probably in someone's tea—bacon, and Cream of Wheat with brown sugar had been prepared—and probably already consumed, since he was usually the last to arrive at the breakfast table.

They had brought fresh croissants and bagels with them from Montreal yesterday. Knowing Yvette's habit of rising early—probably reinforced by her preparation for convent life—he guessed that she had already raided the large freezer in the basement, where such things were kept, to get some croissants, her preferred breakfast food. As the breakfast table rounded into view, he saw that she had also taken out some bagels, John's favourite form of bread at any time of day. So all he had to do was make a fresh pot of tea.

"Going to have some afternoon tea are you, sleepyhead?"

"Be kind to him, Andrew. He might trip over his feet, so soon after getting up, if you upset him."

Whilst John was thumbing through his mental card index, where he had just filed the *bon mot* about the kissing contest for possible future use, in search of a suitable rejoinder, the telephone rang. It was answered by Mrs Cunningham, who had long since given up any hope of changing John's biorhythm. Just as she had accepted Andrew's left-handedness, as something he was born with, she accepted John's morning lethargy (and corresponding evening alertness) as something biological, that it was futile to fight against.

His search having come up with no trenchant retort— other than the ones he had already made use of earlier in the week—John decided not to place an unnecessary load on his grey cells, which had their work cut out for them over the next two days. He pretended not to have heard what his siblings had said.

"Thank you for bringing up the bagels, Yvette."

"She didn't just bring them up for you, Mr van Winkle," said Andrew. "You're not the only person in the family who likes bagels."

"I would like to think that my needs might have been part of the equation."

Mary Cunningham returned at this point. "That was Mrs Moffat. She told me that the monks at the abbey will be holding a choral service this afternoon. And she wondered who your new girl friend was, John."

"So that's who passed us last night."

"Yes. She says she was sorry to have intruded upon your tryst. And ..." continued Mary Cunningham, with a twinkle in her eye, "... of course, she was dying to know who you were embracing."

"Well, I guess we can't keep it a secret any longer," replied John. "Yvette and I are engaged."

To say that Yvette was speechless would be like describing the Second World War as an altercation. She was not only speechless, she was motionless. What the other members of the Cunningham family saw, as they turned to look at her, could have been one of those wax figures at Madame Tousaud's, before the facial colouring had been applied.

"Yes, we are engaged in a wide-ranging discussion about religion, in which Yvette is valiantly, and successfully, holding the fort of orthodox Christianity against the onslaught of barbarous scepticism."

Although the chronicler has not had the opportunity of witnessing such events at first hand, he is prepared to hazard a guess that when Lazarus was awoken from the dead, his facial features underwent a similar progression of changes to that which could now be observed on Yvette's physiognomy.

"Your discussions on this topic appear to have been held at close quarters," ventured John's mother, with a smile.

"Oh, Mrs Cunningham, it was not like that at all!" exclaimed Yvette. "I stumbled on a rock when we were moving to the side of the road and caught hold of John to stop me from falling."

Mrs Cunningham turned to John for confirmation. But before John could say anything, Andrew chimed in. "You don't expect your Mother Superior will believe that, do you, Yvette? By now Mrs Moffat will have told Mrs Stevenson and the ripples will already be half way to Ste Marie d'en Haut."

"Andrew, that was cruel!" Sarah was renowned for her sense of fair play, and she leapt to the defence of her old friend. "You can see how distressed Yvette is." Turning to Yvette, she said "I'm sure Mrs Moffat hasn't been telling anyone else about this, and we'll call her and tell her what happened."

"Being sure about Mrs Moffat's reticence is not something that I would normally venture to be," replied Sarah's mother, smiling. "However, I suspected that she must have misinterpreted something, and asked her not to spread the word until I had spoken to the leading players themselves. I'll call her back and explain the situation to her."

"Before you do, what time was the service this afternoon?" asked John.

"At 4 o'clock, according to Mrs Moffat. But I'd check if you're planning to go. I know they sometimes hold Vespers at 5:30"

The monks at the nearby Abbey of St Luc-du-Lac were respected throughout the Eastern Townships, not only for their bee-keeping, which helped the local farmers with the fertilization of their crops, and provided excellent honey for the Cunninghams' breakfast table, but also for their music. People travelled from far afield to hear them sing Gregorian Chants.

"Isn't it weird that John, who doesn't even believe in God, likes to listen to Church music!" said Sarah.

"What's weird about that?" asked John. "Ancient Egyptian gods and priests play a major role in Verdi's *Aida*, which I enjoy listening to. But I don't believe in Isis and Osiris."

"You're overlooking something important, John," said Yvette. Verdi didn't write *Aida* in praise of the Egyptian gods. They were just a backdrop, like the castles in a fairy tale. Gregorian chants are church liturgy, written in praise of God."

Once again, John was struck by how much fun it would be to spend the rest of his life with someone as keen-witted as Yvette. There would never be a dull moment! And once again he realized the urgency of doing something to change the status quo. As things currently stood, his prospects of enjoying her intellectual—or any other—companionship in the future were dim.

"You're right. I admit it. My answer was too glib. I was too concerned with winning the argument, instead of establishing the truth ..."

"'We have erred and strayed from Thy ways like lost sheep ... and there is no health in us ... have mercy upon us miserable offenders' You're beginning to sound like the Book of Common Prayer!" laughed Andrew, quoting from that venerable book, a leather-bound copy of which each of the Cunningham children had received at their Confirmation.

Andrew was right, of course, John realized. But why did he have to put his oar in, just when an opportunity to praise Yvette for her astuteness—instead of constantly assailing her beliefs—had presented itself?

"Well, what's the answer? Would you deny me the right to enjoy the music because I don't believe in the words?" asked John. "When you sing, along with Elvis,

*Love me tender,*
*Love me dear,*
*Tell me you are mine.*
*I'll be yours through all the years,*
*Till the end of time.*

"Who are you singing to? If you believe the words you are singing, you would appear to be proposing to a woman. Which one?"

Yvette came unexpectedly to John's rescue. "This time, you're right, John. When I sang about Rudolf the Red-nosed Reindeer last night, it certainly wasn't because I believe in such a creature! However, I still feel that there is an essential difference between songs which were never meant to be taken seriously and those that are. Would you be happy singing the words of *La Marseillaise*, for example?"

For the sake of any readers who may not have the words of *La Marseillaise* at their fingertips—or the tips of their tongues—the chorus is reproduced below.

*Aux armes, citoyens!*      *(To arms, citizens!)*
*Formez vos bataillons!*   *(Form your battalions!)*
*Marchons, marchons!*      *(March, march!)*
*Qu'un sang impur* *(May tainted blood)*
*Abreuve nos sillons!*      *(Water our fields!)*

"Whose blood would you like to water your fields with?"

"You're right again. No, I would not be willing to sing *La Marseillaise*. But I can still *listen* to it and find the music stirring. In the same way, I can listen to Bach's

*St Matthew Passion* and find it deeply moving, without necessarily singing along myself.

"What's more, I would enjoy listening to Gregorian chants at the Abbey this afternoon, if you'd care to join me, Yvette."

At last, thought John, those grey cells have managed to get up to speed. He had just asked a prospective nun for a date, in a room full of onlookers, and they had no reason to suspect other motives than purely musical ones. Of course, everything hinged on Yvette's answer.

"Yes. I'd enjoy visiting the Abbey," said Yvette. "But we'd better find out about the time."

"I'd enjoy visiting the Abbey, too," said Sarah.

John loved his sister dearly. She was a sincere, loyal, person, and usually a lot of fun to be with. But there were times, and this was one of them, when he would have liked to strangle her. Figuratively, of course.

"No, Sarah, dear. I need help making the dinner. You can hear the music another time."

John jumped up and hugged his mother. Figuratively, of course.

"Speaking of dinner, Helen and her family are coming. I need some lettuce, tomatoes and a few other things. Who would like to go to Fletcher's and get them for me?"

This time his grey cells were chomping at the bit, and John got in before anyone else had time to reply. "What do you say, Yvette? Would you like to visit Fletcher's Store again, after all these years?"

"Could we walk? We've been indoors so much since we got here. I would enjoy a walk through the winter wonderland outside."

"You could check the time with Jim and Eileen when you're there. I expect they've got a printed notice with the times of all the Abbey services. But be careful not to step on any stones, Yvette," said Mrs Cunningham with a kindly smile. "It won't be so easy to convince Mrs Moffat a second time!"

This time there was no question about it. Yvette did blush. And it was very becoming.

# Chapter 7

## *The Walk to Fletcher's*

It was as if they had fallen down a rabbit hole and ended up inside the picture on one of the Christmas cards adorning the cottage mantelpiece, thought John, who half expected to see a "miniature sleigh and eight tiny reindeer" coming around the next bend. It felt as if every snowflake had been carefully placed to enhance the splendour.

If it wasn't God who had painted this winter landscape with his celestial brush, who had done it? It was difficult for John to conceive that blind accidents of physics could accomplish all this. Could enough monkeys with their typewriters, even working in shifts around the clock, really produce the works of Shakespeare by accident, given enough time?

Yvette in her fur cap and parka looked, well, *beautiful* was the word that blinked like a neon sign in John's brain as he walked beside her on the road which led to Fletcher's General Store. The world was full of attractive young women, all with the additional qualification that he wasn't in love with them, to whom Jesus could have directed his marriage proposal. Why did he have to choose Yvette? On the other hand, John realized, if it hadn't been for this betrothal, he might not have come into contact with Yvette again.

"Have you asked God about the things we were discussing last night before Mrs Moffat interrupted our tête-à-tête?"

"Yes. We have had several conversations."

"And what was the outcome?"

"God doesn't always answer the questions you choose to ask. If He feels there are more important questions, He may answer them instead."

"Which questions did God choose to answer, then?"

"He told me why He has brought me here."

"I could have sworn that I was the one who brought you here, in my car, yesterday. Do you mean that God has been using me as a taxi?"

Yvette could have taken this as sacrilege and reacted angrily. But she didn't. She smiled. An infuriatingly pretty smile.

John's hand went out for the umpteenth time to take hers in his. And for the umpteenth time it stopped short. He had promised.

"He says that he has brought me here to test me. To see whether I can withstand the temptations of the temporal world."

"You mean the way Satan tempted Jesus in the wilderness?"

"Except that the roll He is considering me for cannot begin to compare in importance with that of Christ's."

"So you don't have to fast for 40 days and 40 nights— you get turkey dinner instead?"

Yvette smiled again. Would God approve? Was she passing her test?

"God seems to have come up with a new twist this time. I don't recall that Jesus was tempted with someone of the opposite sex as a life companion."

"I wasn't aware that I had been either," said Yvette, with her mischievous grin.

Confound it! How could anyone so much fun to be with, prefer a cold convent cell to my company? John asked himself yet again.

"You haven't been, actually. It would be foolish of me to propose to someone who was not as interested in becoming my wife as I was in becoming her husband. But it would appear that God is trying to tempt you with that possibility. I guess he reckons that if he can manipulate me into driving a taxi for him, getting me to pop the question to such an attractive woman would be child's play."

Brushing aside the compliment, Yvette replied, "Well since you haven't actually asked me, I won't actually have to turn you down."

At this juncture, both betrothed and unbetrothed pressed themselves against one of the walls of snow lining the road, to let a car pass. Yvette was careful where she placed her feet this time, and took the precaution of putting extra separation between herself and John. This turned out to have been a wise move, for at the wheel of the car which approached them was none other than Mrs Stephenson, whose information-dispersing abilities Andrew has previous hinted at. She smiled—a little too warmly, thought John—and waved as she drove by. Had Mrs Moffat started the rumour mill before Mrs Cunningham had put her straight on the events of last night? He would know soon enough. In this small lake-side community, any new relationship was front-page news.

"I've been thinking about something you said this morning," said John, as they resumed their promenade.

"What was that?"

"You said that in any comparison between Jesus and myself, I would come in second."

"Have you reason to think otherwise?"

"Suppose that we were to hold a contest, and I came out on top, would you be willing to reconsider your decision?"

"I would certainly have to take it into consideration," said Yvette cautiously. "But I can't imagine that the risk is very great. What did you have in mind?"

"I challenge Jesus to a kissing contest. With you as kissing partner and sole judge. Virtual and spiritual kisses don't count. When can we start?"

John felt that the work he had put into storing and cross-referencing this *bon mot* in his mental card index had been worth while.

Yvette smiled again. It was almost getting to be a habit. Would this pull down her marks?

"As sole judge, I'll have to award you that contest by default."

"Are you sure that's what God wants you to do? Perhaps he wants you to hold the contest, so that he can really put you to the test?"

"Get thee behind me, Satan!" replied Yvette resolutely.

"Well then, as victor, I claim my prize, which was to have you reconsider your decision."

"I didn't promise that I would *change* my decision. Only that I would take any victory on your part into consideration."

"And what is the result of your deliberation?"

It is said, perhaps apocryphally, that when the lexicographer Noah Webster's wife happened upon him in the arms of their maid, she exclaimed "Noah, I'm surprised!", to which this paragon of pedantry reportedly replied, "No, my dear. You are amazed. I am surprised."

John was amazed *and* surprised by what happened next. Yvette kissed him.

It was done with military precision: advance, strike, and retreat, before the foe has time to react.

"That was your prize. But my decision remains unchanged."

With the birds still tweeting in his head, John gasped "You seem to be counting on God having a sense of humour."

"Oh, but he does. We often laugh together."

"Has he told you any good jokes lately?"

"We had a little chuckle this morning, after I had brought you your morning tea. We were having a chat, and I remarked on the fact that when I was all yours for the taking, you weren't interested. But now that you can't have me, you want me. God said it reminded Him of a story. It seems there was once this garden full of delicious fruit, in which dwelt a man and his wife. When God told them one day, not to eat a particular fruit, they immediately decided that was the fruit they wanted most of all."

"Did he call you his Miss Forbidden Fruit?"

"*Your* Miss Forbidden Fruit."

John began to realize what he was up against. With the sound of God's chuckles reverberating from its walls, that cloister cell suddenly didn't seem so cold and uninviting. When it came to the interior decoration of monastic living quarters, God could clearly hold his own with the best of them.

"It's funny that God never talked to me that way," said John.

"Perhaps you never talked to him that way."

"It was like talking down a telephone line, with no one at the other end. Maybe he was too busy telling you risqué jokes to bother about me."

"Maybe you had dialled the wrong number?"

"Are you sure that you have dialled the right number? The God who tells you funny stories seems a far cry from the God of the Bible, who is quoted as saying 'I the LORD thy God am a jealous God, visiting the iniquity of the fathers upon the children unto the third and fourth generation of them that hate me'. What chance does that leave a poor sinner? Even if he repents of all his wrongdoings, he still can't go back through four generations and undo the sins of his forefathers."

"I don't talk to God over a telephone line."

"How do you communicate with him, then?"

"Through prayer."

"But how can you be sure that the person who answers your prayers is not an impostor? Have you ever asked him for his identification papers?"

"How can you be sure that Shakespeare is Shakespeare? Shakespeare is the sum total of all the works which bear his name. Which human hand we assign the pen to, changes not one iota of those works. God's name, Yahweh, or Jehovah, means 'I am the One Who Is'. God is whoever answers my prayers."

"Now wait a darned minute! You ain't gonna get away wi' dat smoo' talkin' here."

"What d'ya mean, pardner?"

For the benefit of any readers, who may not have spent the Saturday afternoons of their youth sitting through film matinées, it should be pointed out that this little exchange was a reference to the typical dialogue in cowboy films, which made up the standard fare at such cultural events. For John and Yvette, both of whom had spent innumerable Saturday afternoons thus engaged, this was almost like a second language. Well, third, perhaps.

"Everybody reads the same Shakespeare."

"Everybody reads the same Bible."

"But people don't engage in dialogue with Shakespeare. And if they did, they wouldn't be taken seriously. Anyone trying to justify an action by claiming that 'Shakespeare told me to do this', would not get very far. Yet personal dialogue with God, which no one else has any means of verifying, has led to much blood being spilt.

"If everyone found their prayers answered by the same jolly old elf who seems to have been assigned to your prayer line, the world would be a very different place. But do you really think this can be the same God who answered the prayers of the Spanish Inquisitors, or the combatants in the many wars triggered by the Reformation, who were—on both sides—convinced that God had told them to kill the heretics of the opposing side?"

"I have no way of knowing what God has said to other people in answer to their prayers."

"Isn't that just the point? None of us has any way of knowing what God has supposedly said to anyone else on any matter. How can we possibly have a just society, if religious leaders who claim to have received special instructions from God—which no one else has any means of verifying—are believed and followed in a way that would not be the case if they had told us the truth: that they had come up with their crackpot ideas themselves?"

"The question you are asking me is as if I were to ask you when you are going to stop beating your mother."

"No, it's not. As you well know, I do not beat my mother, or anyone else. But the Catholic Church has burnt people at the stake, precisely because it believed that the ideas they claimed they had received from God were crackpot ideas that they had invented themselves.

"And it's not just a matter of ancient history. Let us suppose that right now a surgeon is operating on a child with abdominal cancer, who is in constant pain. The child stops breathing. The surgeon, a god-fearing man, hears the voice of God saying that it was his will that the patient should be taken out of his pain and his spirit given an express ticket to heaven." John made what he hoped was a dramatic pause.

"And the moral of the story is?"

"Stay tuned. It's coming. Suppose that tomorrow, in the same operating theatre, a different surgeon performs a similar operation on another child. He also hears the voice of God, but this time it tells him to administer artificial ventilation and extra oxygen immediately, with the result that the patient survives the operation, and lives a happy life for another sixty years, before dying peacefully in his sleep.

"Which surgeon heard the 'true' voice of God?"

"That's a hypothetical question."

"Of course it's a hypothetical question. But it's also a matter of life and death."

"I don't have an answer. But I trust in God."

"*Je n'en sçay rien, mais m'actend du tout à Notre-Seigneur.*"

"That's not exactly what I said, but it's a good try."

Yvette was surprised to hear John speaking French. It had taken them about 10 seconds on that ski lift to establish that John's school French was a Chihuahua compared to the Grand Danois of Yvette's English. Although he had spoken French with Yvette's parents out of courtesy, she had found it painful to listen to. She and John had always conversed in English.

"But that *is* exactly what another fair maid, who heard God's voice some 500 years ago, said to the Catholic authorities who were trying her for heresy. Unfortunately, they apparently heard other voices, which instructed them to tie her to a stake and set fire to her."

John considered that the true story of Joan of Arc surpassed any fiction he had ever read. It was all the more remarkable for the excruciating detail of the trial transcripts. To read the exact words spoken in 1431 by the inquisitors, witnesses, and especially Joan herself, put history—and religion—into perspective. It had also had a beneficial effect on his French, bringing it perhaps up to Cocker Spaniel level.

"But that was really a political decision. It was the English who captured her and had her tried."

"Be that as it may, it was an ecclesiastical court that tried her. Many of the witnesses, the Inquisitor and Judge were French clergymen. She was found guilty and executed by officials of the Catholic Church for the sin of heresy."

"But she was later exonerated by the Pope and has since been made a saint."

"So that's all right, then? 'Sorry about the heat, Joan. Please come back, all is forgiven'?"

"Even clergy can make mistakes."

"But God isn't supposed to. God is supposed to be perfect. However, the important point is that, even if God exists, and even if he is perfect, we have no reliable way of communicating with him. I assume that the priest who pronounced the death sentence on Joan prayed to God for guidance, just as the Pope who later exonerated her did. Yet one of them heard God say 'Kill her', whereas the other heard him say 'She's innocent.' If the church authorities can't agree amongst themselves on what God has said, how can we ordinary mortals ever hope to?

"This is not a one-off accident, either. History is full of cases where one party has heard God order them to kill another party. Galileo was threatened with the same fate as Joan, unless he renounced his belief that the Earth revolves around the sun and is therefore not the centre of the universe. Galileo did renounce it, and his life was spared. Much later God told the Church authorities that Galileo had been right all along. Surely an omniscient God should have got that right in the first place?"

"I have no answers. But I have faith"

# Chapter 8

## *Fletcher's General Store*

Fletcher's General Store was an integral part of the Lake Gomareph community. Generations of lakeside families had done their shopping there. And generations of Fletcher's had served them faithfully. It was strategically situated at the juncture of three roads, one of them skirting the shores of Lake Gomareph, a second leading to the ski hill, the third leading to the nearest town, and beyond that the highway to Montreal. The only other building nearby was the farmhouse across the road, owned by a brother of Jim and Eileen Fletcher, the current proprietors of the store.

It was a common mistake for newcomers and casual visitors to Lake Gomareph to assume that Jim and Eileen were husband and wife. But that was not the case. Jim was married to the editor of the local newspaper, *The Township Times*, whereas Eileen, it was often said, was married to the store.

Although John had a vague recollection of Jim and Eileen's parents standing behind the counter when he was a child, it was the friendly face and good-natured banter of Eileen Fletcher that John—and all the other "regulars"— associated with the store today. So much so, that in local parlance people often talked of "going to Eileen's" for a bag of flour, much to the chagrin of her brother, Jim, who's indefatigable efforts as butcher, buyer, stockist, and on-the-shelf-putter, freed Eileen to serve—and entertain—their customers.

"Hullo, Yvette! We haven't seen you in these parts for a while."

Eileen was renowned for her memory. Not only did she remember the names of her customers, many of whom she saw only a few times a year during their annual holidays, but she remembered their likes and dislikes and the things they had talked about.

Her memory was also an essential part of the book-keeping system, a prominent feature of which was a shoe box, in which Eileen kept the bills run up by her customers When children came in to buy things for their parents, she always knew which bill to put it on. And, it must be said, she sometimes fiddled the accounts, by weighing liquorice pipes and gum drops together with the tomatoes and cheese—on the strict understanding that these items were to be consumed before reaching home. Not that many parents were fooled. A goodly number of them had received the same kickbacks from Jim & Eileen's parents when they were children, much to the delight of their respective dentists.

"So you're the mystery sweetheart John was spotted with last night! I'm happy to see you two back together again. I've always said so: John is a young man with good taste."

Yvette turned to John, and he didn't let her down.

"Who has been spreading that rumour, Eileen?"

"I guess at this point everybody's doing their bit to pass it around. Why? Don't try and tell me it isn't true. I can see in your eyes that you are fond of this young lady."

"Your powers of observation are unsurpassed, Eileen. I won't try to deny it. However, Yvette has other plans. Next week she will be forsaking the pleasures of this world and entering the convent of Ste Marie d'en Haut. What Mrs Chatterbox saw when she drove by last night, was Yvette catching hold of me to stop her from falling. We had moved to the side of the road to let Chatterbox past, and Yvette tripped on something under the snow."

Eileen was a woman with a heart the size of a house. She could see how distressed Yvette was over all this, and determined to do what she could to put matters right.

"Poor Yvette! Don't worry, sweetheart. You've come to the right person to straighten things out," said Eileen with a smile of encouragement. "The question is, should we put an article in *The Township Times*, stick a poster in the store window, or rely on word of mouth—my mouth?"

"Thank you, Eileen. I can think of no more competent hands—or mouth—to leave this matter in."

Younger readers may not be familiar with the work of Norman Rockwell, whose paintings adorned the covers of *The Saturday Evening Post* for several decades. Such readers will have to take it on faith, that the picture which greeted everyone who walked through the door of Fletcher's General Store could have been lifted straight from the front cover of that venerable publication. It was like stepping back in time. There were shelves from floor to ceiling, laden with everything a cottage dweller could conceivably need. There were lids and lifters for your wood stove, flat irons that you heated on the stove, and oil lanterns—so essential during the blackouts, which occurred in winter when power lines collapsed under the weight of accumulated ice, and in summer during thunderstorms.

Since the upper shelves were only accessible by climbing a wooden ladder, a natural system of stock rotation had evolved, whereby items that were less frequently sought after gradually got promoted to higher and higher shelves. This had resulted in the top shelf becoming a sort of museum, where things that nobody had asked for during the past generation gathered dust. There were tin boxes that contained, or had contained, mustard powder, sulphur ointment, cigarettes, and tyre repair kits. In addition there were coffee mills that you turned by hand, a jug and basin for your bedside table, a large timetable for trains which had long ago ceased to run, and many other things, some of which John was unable to identify.

John and Yvette filled their basket from the lower shelves and returned with it to the counter.

"Turkey à la King, tonight is it?" asked Eileen, as she emptied the basket and totted up the bill with her wooden pencil.

"Now how could you possibly figure that out, Eileen?" asked John incredulously.

"Peas, cream, mushrooms—and the fact that your mother bought a turkey a couple of days ago," replied Eileen, laughing.

Even Yvette had recovered enough to smile. And to remember about the monastery.

"Eileen, do you know when the monks will be singing this evening?"

"Goodness, don't they sing vespers every evening? Is there something special today? Have a look in the post office. There's a notice there with the times of their services."

The "post office" Eileen referred to was at the other end of the long counter, between the ice-cream freezer and the chocolate bars. Taped on the side of the freezer was a picture of the Abbey of St Luc-du-Lac, and below it the times of services. For today the message was "4 p.m., choral vespers. Visitors welcome."

It had begun to snow again, as they made their way back towards the cottage. John and Yvette walked on in silence for a while. Although we can only speculate as to what thoughts were going through the mind of the fairer member of this twosome, we can be in no doubt as to what subject John's grey cells were currently concentrating on.

Ever since they had rubbed the sleep out of their eyes this morning, they had made it abundantly clear to him that a) he was in love with Yvette, b) Yvette was not in love with him, and c) he had very little time to effect a change in b).

They had pointed out to him the advantage of no longer having to feel inhibited. Since he was now prepared to offer Yvette the alternative of his hand in marriage, he no longer needed to worry about robbing her of her faith.

At any rate, he didn't need to worry as much. Parallel with his gradual loss of faith in the God of the Bible, John had come to the realization that there is more to religion than which gods you believe in. Take away religion, and you won't necessarily have a better world.

If you want to improve living conditions for slum dwellers, you don't begin by tearing down their ramshackle dwellings, however wretched these may be. The first step is to build something better for them to move into. John was acutely aware that, as yet, he didn't have anything better to offer.

Even if people no longer believed in God, there is no shortage of other superstitions on offer: everything from astrology to communism. Wasn't it G K Chesterton who said, "When people stop believing in God, they don't believe in nothing, they believe in anything"?

But more important, in John's view, than which fairy tales people chose to believe in, was religion's social roll. He agreed with his mother, that religion is the cohesive force in our society, and is what prevents us from going around shooting one another. A society in which right is whatever you can get away with, and wrong is when you get caught, was not the kind of society that he wanted to be instrumental in bringing about.

For this reason, John was a very non-strident atheist— if atheist is what he was. Within the family, of course, there was no way that he could keep his world-view secret. Nor would he have wanted to. The openness with which these things could be discussed in the Cunningham household was a source of great comfort to him. But outside the family, he was reluctant to challenge the beliefs of good people, whom he felt would only be the poorer if he succeeded in depriving them of their faith.

There was, however, one fatal flaw in this reasoning. It didn't take into account the fact that the only way he was going to win the hand of the good person walking beside him, was by challenging her beliefs head on.

Whilst mulling this over in his mind, he had become aware of a feeling of unease. It began as an undefined sense of something not being the way it should be, as if he had forgotten to turn off the stove. Just as he had come to the conclusion that it had something to do with the way Yvette was walking, she addressed him.

"John, I'm going to have to dash into the bushes. You keep walking, and I'll catch up to you." With that she climbed over the snow bank at the side of the road and began to bulldoze a path through the snow towards the nearest trees.

John did as suggested. If he had hung around waiting, he would have drawn the attention of any passers by to the activities taking place on the other side of the snow bank. Although it had taken him completely by surprise, now that he had the leisure to reflect on it, he realized that, of course, even nuns had to answer the calls of nature. In fact, although it is not recorded in the Bible, even Jesus must have had to attend to such matters—at any rate if he was 100% human. Is it possible that at this very moment, in a mountain cave somewhere in Palestine, there are divine coprolites waiting to be analysed by some future palaeontologist? For some reason, this struck John as a very irreverent idea.

Something else struck John a few minutes later. On the back of his head.

He turned around, and saw nothing. To be sure, there was lots of snow, an assortment of trees, some almost-covered-over tyre tracks, and his own footprints. But nothing that could account for the sensation he had just experienced in the back of his head. There were no trees close enough for playful chipmunks to sit in and throw nuts at him. Besides, that only happened in the cartoons they used to show before the main film at Saturday matinées. Real-life chipmunks would be catching up on their sleep at this time of year, and anyway they wouldn't be throwing away their valuable nuts in mid-winter.

John looked up. Could a careless Snowy Owl have dropped a lemming on him? There was no sign of any fowl in the sky. Nor of any lemming on the ground. John resumed his leisurely perambulation. Could he possibly have suffered a stroke? He had always associated strokes with elderly patients, who were overweight, smoked, drank a lot, had high blood pressure, or for some other reason failed to attain top marks on their medical examinations.

As his thoughts were thus engaged, a fur cap and ponytail caught up with him.

"I hope you didn't feel embarrassed," said Yvette, looking a bit embarrassed herself.

"Me? Isn't that your job?"

Yvette looked a bit more embarrassed. But there was something else. A stranger wouldn't have noticed it. But John had known Yvette long enough to recognize a *soupçon* of that mischievous glint in her eye.

"I think God tried to tell me something whilst you were away," said John.

"Oh?" said Yvette, interestedly. "What did he say?"

"It never got that far. He tapped me on the head to get my attention, but when I turned around, he had gone. I might say, he doesn't tap lightly!"

"Perhaps he was just reminding you of his existence, since you seem to have been a bit unclear on that point recently."

"Perhaps. But there is another possibility." John watched Yvette closely. "Tell me, are nuns allowed to throw snowballs?"

There are some people who should never play poker. They can no more bluff than they can rotate their ears in opposite directions. Yvette was one of those people. Her cheeks took on a healthy reddish hue.

"It would be interesting to see your score card at this point," said John. "After watching you throw that snowball, and duck down behind the snow bank so that I wouldn't see you, even a God who chuckles would find it hard to check the yes-box beside the question 'Does she show sufficient detachment from the frivolities of earthly life?'"

"Don't you think that God would let me have one last fling, before I forswear the carnal world? After all, I will be able to serve him better, if I have practical experience of the temptations of the flesh."

"That wasn't the attitude you took towards the kissing contest. No striving for practical experience there!"

"Ah, but I already have practical experience in that regard. Otherwise I wouldn't have been so ready to award you victory by walkover."

John wondered if he should take this as a compliment, and if so, whether it meant that he was still in there with a chance.

"Have you ever tried suggesting to your priests, that they might be in a better position to advise their flock, if they had practical experience of bringing up a family?"

"The Church has decided that its clergy can better concentrate on serving the Lord if it is not distracted by earthly cares. 'He that is unmarried careth for the things that belong to the Lord ... But he that is married careth for the things that are of the world'."

"But isn't the primary job of the clergy to care for some very important 'things that are of the world'—namely their parishioners, who turn to them for guidance?

"Picture an ad in the newspaper: 'Jim's Marriage Counselling. Entrust your marital problems to a confirmed bachelor, guaranteed untarnished by personal experience of married life.' How much credibility would you be prepared to give to Jim?"

"But you can't compare a marriage counsellor with a priest! A priest receives God's guidance."

"We've seen what happened to Joan of Arc, when God guided the clergy at her trial. I think I'd prefer to take my chances with Jim.

"Don't you find it even mildly absurd that, for the best part of 2000 years, the ultimate authorities on sex and child rearing for millions of Catholics have been unmarried men with no experience whatsoever of either of these matters— unless they obtained it illicitly?"

"Well, I sincerely hope that Jim is able to help you with your marriage problems, John."

Yvette said this with a touch of irony in her voice, but without any hint of mischievousness in her eyes. In fact, she said it like a nun. For the first time, John *could* picture her in a habit.

Had he been too derisive? It was a difficult middle course that he was trying to steer. If he was too disrespectful of her religion, it would turn her against him—which may, indeed, already have happened. Yet if he didn't succeed in shaking her faith in that religion, she would end up as a nun. In either case, he would lose her.

"I sense that you have given up on me. Poor sinner, he is destined to 'be tormented with fire and brimstone ... for ever and ever', or words to that effect, appear to be going through your mind."

"I was asking God to forgive your arrogance, John, and I was also praying that you may be saved. It's never too late to repent."

This could have been Sr Marguerite, OSB (formerly Yvette Dumont of Montreal, Quebec) talking, thought John.

# Chapter 9

## The Walk Home

What did nuns wear in sub-zero temperatures? They couldn't very well stay indoors all winter. Did they have fur-lined habits? Thick woolly undergarments?

Whatever they wore, speculated John, as he and Yvette scrambled over a snow bank to let the snowplough pass, it couldn't be as pretty as the red parka and fur cap that Yvette was wearing now. Nor would there be any saucy pony tail bobbing along behind.

How could anyone so pretty, and obviously intelligent, decide to devote the rest of her life to the contemplation of imaginary beings? How could she not feel the same urge to take him in her arms that he felt towards her?

John was struck again by the power religious beliefs can exercise on seemingly rational human beings. From the dawn of civilization, humans have been sacrificing other humans to their various gods. Nor was this something that had long ago been committed to the rubbish dump of human history. John still shuddered whenever he recalled that, even today, all three major monotheistic religions revere as one of their founding fathers, a man who was prepared to slit the throat of his own son, because he thought he had heard a voice telling him to do so.

People were willing to kill and to die for their religious beliefs. Joan of Arc was only the most famous of the many people who allowed themselves to be burnt alive rather than renounce some religious idea they had.

If Yvette had been born in Mecca, would she still be planning to shut herself away in a Christian monastery? In all probability she wouldn't even have been taught to read, and the only God she would know about would be a very different personage from the one she now planned to devote the rest of her life to, and with a completely different set of rigid laws. It was all in her head. He was being turned down for a blasted superstition!

Was the battle lost? The more he argued against the existence of the God she believed in, the more defensive Yvette became of that God, and the more seemingly determined to leave the profane world—the one in which John had his headquarters—behind her.

Actually, this didn't come as a complete surprise. John was well aware that, back in the days when he was a believer, he had reacted the same way, whenever anyone had attacked his God. Even now that he had stopped believing in God, his gut reaction was to find faults in atheist arguments. His gradual abandonment of belief in God had come about solely by finding holes in what religious believers themselves had said and written.

During his God-fearing youth, whenever he had found some dogma incomprehensible, he had brushed it aside for the time being, thinking that "someone up there", some priest or knowledgeable author, understood it, and would be able to explain it to him, if he just took the time to discuss it with them or read what they had written.

It wasn't until he started taking the time to do so, that he began to realize that they no more understood the 'Mysteries' of the Immaculate Conception, Virgin Birth, Vicarious Atonement, Trinity, and the like, than he did himself. He had finally come to the conclusion that *there is no one in the whole world who understands these things.* If anyone did, they would no longer be mysteries. The Christian Church is a house built on sand. Quicksand. It swallows its believers whole.

As they climbed over the—now higher—wall of snow back onto the road, John wondered if he should try to propound some Christian doctrine instead, and see if Yvette would find fault with it, as he had done. Perhaps he could have a sudden conversion, like that of Saul on the road to Damascus. Would the prospect of a Christian prophet as husband change Yvette's mind?

Although he would have been prepared to put up with the discomfort of falling to the road and getting snow down his neck, he realized that he would never be able to pull it off. It wasn't just that the 'light from heaven' would be hard to fake, but honesty was fundamental to his being. Even though he no longer believed that God might throw him into 'a lake of fire' if he told a lie, there was something inside him that wouldn't let him do it. Even if it meant losing Yvette.

For no reason at all, other than a sense of frustration, John scooped up some snow and made a snowball. Since it was well below freezing, he had to press hard to get the snow to stick together. He idly remembered learning about that in his high-school Physics class: compression produces heat, which melts the snow. It also melts the ice under skates, so that they actually glide along on a thin film of lubricating water. Or so their teacher had told them. He debated throwing the snowball at Yvette, or even putting it down her neck, but decided that wouldn't be a gentlemanly thing to do. He had promised.

On an impulse, John took out his pocket knife, cut the snowball in half, and placed the halves beside one another on the snow bank left by the plough at the side of the road. He then took two steps backwards, solemnly raised his arms, and uttered the words "Verily, verily, what man hath joined together, God hath put asunder".

Yvette, who had watched these proceedings with increasing incredulity, said "What on earth are you talking about, John? God hasn't put your snowball asunder. I watched you do it with your pocket knife."

"I was using the snowball as a symbol for our relationship."

"In that case I don't think much of your symbolism. God had nothing to do with rending our *former* relationship asunder. You broke it off yourself."

"You're right. I should have said 'What man hath put asunder, God intendeth to keep that way'"

Of course, Yvette was right. This was all nonsense. John's brain had been working overtime, and he was beginning to feel shell-shocked.

Yet the fact remained that unless a major change took place in Yvette's beliefs within the next twenty-four hours or so, she would don her habit next week and that would be the end of that. John decided to have another go. The worst that could happen was that Yvette would continue with her current plans.

"You accused me of arrogance a few minutes ago. But which is more arrogant: to claim that you know the mind of God, and what he wants us to do, or to use the mind that God has given us—assuming that he has—to think things through for ourselves?"

"God has also given us guidelines such as the Bible, Jesus and the Saints, to help us in our thinking."

"So we are free to think, as long as we reach the conclusions God wants us to. Is that the extent of our free will?"

"God puts no restriction on what we may think and do. But we must bear the consequences of our choices."

"Then God is a sadist."

"How can you say that?"

"The very existence of hell and its bonfires, is proof enough. Hell has no other purpose than to incinerate humans who displease God in some way, so-called sinners."

"But God hopes that man will not sin."

"In that case, why doesn't he design us so that we don't sin? He has already shown us that he knows how to do it. According to the Bible Jesus was without sin. Yet God continues to create us imperfect humans in the full knowledge that he will end up throwing some of us onto the bonfire and watching us sizzle. If that's not sadism, what is?"

"Jesus came into the world to save sinners. He wants to save us all"

"Save us from what?"

"Damnation"

"You mean save us from being thrown onto the bonfire. If Jesus really wants to save us all, why doesn't he just put out the fire?"

"It pains me to hear you talking about the God of Love that way."

"Which God?"

"The Bible tells us 'God is love'"

"It couldn't have been out of any love for us that God created us. We weren't around to be loved. Not even God can love what doesn't exist. He might possibly have created us because he wanted someone to love, and to be loved by in return. But in that case it is just as ridiculous for him to throw those of his creatures which displease him into the fire, as it is for a child to get angry with one of her toys and break it."

"But He came into the world and was crucified for our sake. Jesus died for us. Surely there can be no greater demonstration of love than laying down your life to save others."

"Throwing people into fires is one of the least convincing expressions of love that I have come across. If God is unhappy with our behaviour, why doesn't he redesign us, so that we do what he wants us to, instead of behaving like a spoilt child who is displeased with its toy?

"The God of the Bible is trying to force us to love him, and threatens us with hellfire if we don't. That's as if I should say to you, 'Love me, or I'll kill you!'"

"Instead you say, 'Love me, or I'll insult your God,'" replied Yvette. The mischievous glint was back in her eyes.

Damn it! There, he'd said it. Why does such a delectable creature want to isolate herself from the world? More to the point: why does such a delectable female want to isolate herself from his company?

"I apologize, Yvette. I did not set out to insult your God. Many of the finest people I know are sincere Christians, and I'm convinced that belief in God has a beneficial effect on our society. But I don't see how I can get you to give up this inane idea of locking yourself away in a monastery unless I can shake your belief."

"You could try asking me," said Yvette demurely.

To say that John was dumbfounded doesn't really do justice to the whirlwind that swept through his mind, ripping up his thoughts willy-nilly, and depositing them, bruised and torn, far from their original contexts. Ask her. Yes, of course, he could ask her. Why hadn't he thought of that? Just wait until he got home. Those grey cells were going to get a talking to that they wouldn't soon forget!

After first ensuring that there were no approaching cars, or snowploughs, John knelt down on the road and took Yvette's hand.

"Dear Yvette, I love you. Please reconsider your decision to become a nun."

Yvette tapped him on the shoulder with her hand and said "Rise up, Sir John."

"Gosh, that was quick work! From nun to queen in 5 seconds flat."

Yvette smiled. However, it was not one of those broad smiles that said all was right with the world. It was one of those faint smiles that said "Yes, but ..."

"If I don't enter the convent now, I will have to wait until next autumn. Programs for postulants are only run twice a year. What would you have to say to me during the next six months, that you can't say now?"

"I could tell you how much you mean to me."

"Would it take you six months to tell me that?" laughed Yvette. You seem to have managed quite well without me for the past 5 years. I'm sure that you will be able to do so in the future as well."

Yvette had, of course, every right to take him to task. He could hardly have expected her to hang around waiting for him to signal that he had changed his mind, after he had unceremoniously dumped her five years ago.

"Go ahead. Rub it in. But you told me a while ago that it was never too late to repent our sins. Are you going to be less generous than God, and not accept my change of heart?"

"It's a question of what your 'change of heart' involves. As I understand it, you evolutionary biologists consider that love, and all emotions, are just a case of chemical reactions in our brains. What's to prevent you from having a different chemical reaction the next time you happen to see a pretty girl? You appear already to have had several different such reactions with respect to me."

John realized that he was in hot water here. Yvette had every reason to question his commitment, in light of his past behaviour. In fact, he would have thought less of her if she hadn't. But that didn't change the fact that he wanted her now more than anything in the world.

"You're not prepared to accept my word as a gentleman?" It was a thin straw to grasp at. But Yvette was the one who had made it a condition for coming to Lake Gomareph.

"What's it worth? When your parents married, they vowed to 'live together after God's ordinance in the holy estate of matrimony', to love, honour and keep one another, in sickness and in health, forsaking all others, so long as they both should live. This was a vow made before God, which meant something to them."

"You mean they would be afraid to break it, lest they should end up on the bonfire?"

"You seem to be fixated with this idea of bonfires. The marriage service contains no reference to hell or to fires. But it contains many references to the benefits of marriage for man and wife, for children, and for society.

"When you were growing up, I'm sure that your parents had occasion to punish you from time to time. I can't picture you as a little saint."

"I think my parents would be inclined to agree with you on that point."

"Do you consider that your parents were sadists because they punished you? Would they have been able to do as good a job of bringing up you children, if they hadn't let it be known that there was an unpleasant punishment lurking in the background if you seriously misbehaved?"

"But the punishment was always such that there was no question of our not surviving. At no point did they even threaten to throw us onto a fire."

"The Bible uses imagery that we humans can understand. Do you remember what your mother said about Ron? When he was a puppy, there would have been no use in asking him politely not to pee on the carpet. But when you threatened to swat him if he did, he understood. As a result, he learned how to live in a house and became a dearly loved member of the family.

"If you were to make a marriage vow, what would it mean to you? 'I vow to stay with you until my next chemical reaction'? If God doesn't exist in your world, then vowing 'to live together after God's ordinance in the holy estate of matrimony' must be just meaningless mumbo jumbo to you.

"If I were to marry you, each time you introduced me to one of your female friends, how would I know that I wasn't shaking hands with one of your lovers?"

"If you mean sexual lovers, you would know, because I haven't had any. I believe in the sanctity of marriage."

At this point forgetful readers may wish to refer to Chapter 2, where Yvette's classical training was briefly mentioned.

"Sanctity? Do you know what that word means? It comes from the Latin *sanctus*, meaning 'holy', the same root that 'saint' comes from. To what God or gods do you hold marriage to be holy?"

"All right. I believe in the inviolability of marriage."

"Until your next chemical reaction?"

"Now it's your turn to be fixated. I haven't said anything about chemical reactions. You have been putting words in my mouth."

"But have I been doing so unfairly? If you have abstained from sexual activity, I can only assume that it is a vestige of your Christian upbringing that has held you back. I can't imagine there is anything in your biology books that would restrain you."

"Not in my biology books. But in my moral code. I have not abandoned my morals, just because I have stopped believing in God."

"But how can I, or anyone else, possibly know what's in your personal moral code? You know, because I am a committed Christian, what moral code you can expect me to adhere to. But I don't have the foggiest notion what code you may have pieced together, and even if I did, what's to keep you from changing it tomorrow?

"Moral codes aren't like ice-cream flavours, where your personal preferences don't affect anyone else. They're like driving a car. Even if it's nice for you yourself to know what side of the road you will be driving on, so that you don't have to make a new decision each time you turn a corner, it's even nicer for oncoming drivers to know which side of the road they can expect you to stay on."

"I would like to think that we could build our society around a code of moral conduct that we agreed on and adhered to, not because God threatened to throw us into hell fires if we didn't, but because we had decided ourselves that it was good for us to do so."

"Well, John, I wish you luck in building your new society, and I sincerely hope that you will find someone who can accept your inviolable marriage vows. But I'm not that person.

"And anyway, God has called me to become a nun."

John hadn't been keeping accurate score. But he guessed that at this point it was about: God 12 – J Cunningham 1. The kissing contest was his only victory so far.

They turned down the cottage drive and a yellow meatball came galloping up to greet them.

# Chapter 10

## The Abbey Church & Drive Back

As he sat beside Yvette on the hard wooden pews of St Luc-du-Lac Abbey church, surrounded by stone walls, vaulted ceilings, stained-glass windows, and an assortment of other religious symbols, John could feel almost 2000 years of Christian tradition rushing in on him. The bells were ringing from the steeple, announcing that vespers were about to begin. First the tolling of a solitary bell; then a second was added; then a third; until finally four bells of different pitches were sending their message out over the countryside; and to the little congregation assembled below.

The Abbey church was almost full. As John watched new arrivals first kneel in silent prayer, then sit back and smile at their neighbours, he felt a strong sense of loneliness. Here were all these good people, secure in their beliefs, happy with their lot, ready to pitch in and help one another at a moment's notice—*and he didn't belong.*

Wouldn't it be easier for him just to forget about the dogma and join the club? Even if he didn't actually believe in God, was that really necessary? After all, he believed in the Christian moral code, and that was surely more important? What's more, if his "reconversion" happened soon enough, he might be able to prevent Yvette from throwing her life away.

The bells stopped ringing, and the monks processed in, chanting *Deus, in auditorium meum intende.* As they reached their places around the altar, they fell silent. Then they began an antiphon, *Fidelia omnia mandata eius*, the

Abbot chanting every second verse on his own, the other monks responding with the following verse in unison.

Gregorian chant isn't something you can do in your living room. It needs stone walls and high ceilings to echo off. And it needs monks to sing it. As John watched the brown-clad monks performing their religious rituals, he was reminded of beavers building a dam. Just as dam-building is somehow programmed into the beavers' genes, Gregorian chant and stone walls seem to be an expression of what it is to be a monk.

As a biologist, John would have been interested to know that, many years later, another biologist, Richard Dawkins, would elaborate on this idea in his book *The Extended Phenotype*. But unfortunately, we have no way of telling him.

Another thing that John, the biologist, had speculated over was the effect Gregorian chant has on listeners, even if they don't understand a word of Latin. Just as it is impossible to remain indifferent to the cries of a human baby, the chanting of monks seems to appeal to some basic instinct within us. It seems to say "Relax, forget about the world outside, there is nothing else you should be doing right now, close your eyes, let yourself be engulfed by eternity."

Thus engulfed, John's relaxed mind tried to figure out which modes the chants were being sung in. Today our Western music is written almost entirely in either major or minor keys. However, this is a relatively recent development. Throughout the Middle Ages, music could be written in any of six "authentic" modes, corresponding to the all-white-note piano scales starting on D, E, F, G, A or C, the respective modes being numbered I, III, V, VII , IX, and XI. Only IX and XI—our minor and major scales, respectively—are used in modern music. Each of these modes is as distinct from the others as a minor key is from a major.

John knew this because he had read about it in *The Oxford Companion to Music*. That book, slightly longer than the Bible, was the work of one man, Percy Alfred Scholes. John had long ago decided that if he were ever to be confined to a dessert island, and were only allowed to have one book with him, this would be it. Seldom had he managed to look something up without being enticed by Scholes's wit and insight, and his extensive collection of illustrations, to spend half an hour or more following cross-references to other interesting topics.

One topic that he had happened upon in this way was that of birdsong. As Scholes pointed out, birds and humans seem to be Nature's only musicians. Scholes compared bird song, passed on through the generations, but subject to modification, with human folk song, passed on in similar fashion. Scholes speculated that some birds seem to appreciate music for its own sake, singing as they do even when they are not trying to attract a mate. It appears that some birds are even aware of such things as octaves and triads. Another interesting observation was that birds with spectacular plumage are seldom the best singers, which echoed John's own observation that humans who display the most highly developed talents are seldom the best looking—since the latter can usually get ahead without unduly exerting themselves.

When it came to composers, Scholes didn't just present dry-as-dust dates of birth and death, and lists of works. He told you about the things that mattered, not least the things that had inspired composers to write their great works. John's enjoyment of *Symphonie Fantastique* had taken on a whole new dimension after reading the account of Berlioz's turbulent love life.

Berlioz seemed to have pursued women, thought John, much as a dog chases a car. Just as a dog wouldn't know what to do with a car if it ever caught one, Berlioz seemed to loose interest in the objects of his desire once he had managed to capture them. His passion was apparently for love itself, rather than for the women to whom he directed his love. Nonetheless, that passion had inspired him to write music such as will be played as long as there are people left on this planet to be enraptured by it.

John would have been saddened to learn that, although this book would still be in print half a century later, the red pen of Political Correctness would have expurgated all the interesting asides that so delighted him. No latter-day Robinson Crusoe would be likely to pack the contemporary edition of this work in his bags, before setting off for his dessert island. But this is another thing we have no means of telling John about—nor, in this case, any reason to.

Yvette's mind was clearly occupied with thoughts of a different nature. She was not an onlooker who, like John, had come to listen to the music. She was a participant, who had come to commune with her God. Throughout the service she whispered the words, which she seemed to know off by heart; she knew when to kneel in prayer without waiting to see what other people were doing; and she appeared to be oblivious to John's presence. She was, thought John, to all intents and purposes already a nun, who just happened to be wearing civilian clothes—and a very un-nun-like pony-tail.

As John watched her, he pictured her in his mind wearing a habit, and realized that, barring a last-minute miracle, this is probably the way he would remember Yvette for the rest of his life.

The Abbot chanted his benediction and the monks filed out. Yvette's face glowed with a radiance that exceeded anything he had seen in the days when she had been in love with him.

"I'm thinking about becoming a Christian again," said John thoughtfully, as he navigated the car over the snow-covered road leading back towards Lake Gomareph.

"Thinking about it?" asked Yvette. "Do you think about falling in love?"

"What do you mean?"

"Did you have to think about it, before you decided you were in love with me? Surely, either you *are* in love, or you aren't. It's not something you decide to be through rational thought. Neither can you "decide" to be a Christian. Either you believe in Jesus and *are* a Christian, or you don't believe in Jesus and you aren't."

John felt as if Yvette had whipped out her six-shooters, fired two shots at him from point blank range, twirled the guns around her fingers, and was now replacing them in their holsters. Yes, he had thought about it, before deciding he was in love with her—for the second time. No, he did not believe in Jesus as anything other than an ordinary human being. But did this make Yvette right?

"Do you mean that back in the days when you said you were in love with me, it was just some sort of primeval urge that attracted you to me? Had you not thought though what a lifetime living with me might entail?" asked John.

"Of course I thought about it. What's more, I liked what I saw. But that came afterwards. I wouldn't have bothered thinking about it, if I hadn't been in love with you to start with."

"Suppose that you had married me, and after a few years, when everything had become routine, you had come to the realization that the passionate love which had attracted you to me was gone. Wouldn't you feel that we still had a commitment to each other, and that even without the passion, there was still a lot which united us—and we could add to that as the years went by, if we worked at it."

"That is the point of marriage. The love between husband and wife, which begins as passion, matures into a love based on loyalty—the same kind of love we have for our parents, brothers and sisters."

"Isn't the same thing possible with religion? Suppose I no longer believe in the magic of supernatural beings, but feel a strong sense of loyalty towards other Christians, and believe in the Christian code of ethics. Isn't it better that I remain within the Christian Church, instead of 'divorcing' myself from it? I could refrain from giving voice to my scepticism."

"Do you really think that you could fool God?"

"I wasn't thinking of trying to fool God. I thought that we could come to an agreement, whereby I wouldn't argue against his existence, and he would exonerate me from saying the creed in church."

Yvette smiled. "I can hear someone laughing in the background."

"So I'm just a joke as far as you and God are concerned?"

If we had been able to interrupt the story at this point, to ask John how he thought Yvette would respond to this question, it is unlikely that he would have been able to give us the correct answer—even if we had given him six guesses, instead of the customary three.

Yvette put her hand on John's arm.

"I'm very touched that you would consider going to such lengths for my sake, John. But do you really think you could go through with it? What would you do when the dinner table conversation turned to God? Say 'No comment'? Suppose we were to have children, and they asked you about God, what would you tell them? What would you tell your own conscience?"

Yvette may have been touched emotionally by John's devotion. But John was now being touched physically by Yvette. Even if a fur-lined glove, an insulated parka, a woolly jumper and a cotton shirt intervened, this was the first time in five years that Yvette had actually touched him as an expression of her feeling towards him. That quick peck on the cheek during the kissing contest this morning didn't count.

How many heavens were there? Was it seven, or eleven? It didn't matter how many there used to be. John had just been transported to a new one, on top of all the old ones. Miles above the old ones.

In fact, he came close to transporting them both to heaven. During the events we have just been eavesdropping on, John's concentration on his driving, if we were to measure it on a numerical axis, had moved into negative territory.

His concentration suddenly raced along that axis in the positive direction, as he realized that they were travelling altogether too fast, and were approaching a curve that cut off his view of oncoming traffic.

By the time the African drum had stopped beating time inside his chest and he felt he had things under control again, Yvette had long since removed her hand. But that didn't matter. He had heard her say it: "Suppose we were to have children". It was something that she could at least contemplate. Furthermore, it wasn't any dislike for him that stood in the way. It was her blasted belief in God.

"You're right, of course." said John, trying not to let Yvette know how close to being united with her fiancé she had just been. "I couldn't go through the rest of my life without being able to open my mouth on theological matters. But is it really necessary for a husband and wife to agree on all things religious? After all, one of them could change his or her views at some later date. Isn't it better if they are able to discuss these matters openly?"

"That might well be a good arrangement for some people. But the thought of waking up beside an atheist every morning has no appeal for me, when I could instead be serving God."

Here we were, back at square one, thought John. Nothing he had said had made any difference, and the time was fast approaching when he would have to wish Yvette all happiness in the life she had chosen, and say goodbye. For ever and ever, amen.

But not before he had had another go.

"Did you hear God laughing in church, when I was having these thoughts about reconversion?"

"No. Your thoughts in church were a private matter between you and God, and none of my business. But when you brought me into the discussion, God was able to share his amusement with me."

"Isn't that a violation of both our free wills?"

"Why should it be?"

"I certainly didn't ask God to share our negotiations with anyone else. Have you asked him to eavesdrop on my thoughts for you?"

"God didn't reveal your thoughts to me. You did! I have told God that I wish to be his servant, and he has my consent to do whatever he wants to with me. So he is not violating my free will when he shares a joke with me— provided he does not divulge anyone else's secrets which, of course, he would never do."

"Did Lazarus give Jesus his consent to be raised from the dead?"

"He may have asked for God's help before he died. Or he may have asked God to intervene after he died. We have no way of knowing these things. Nor does it matter. We know that other people asked for God's help on his behalf."

"So God can violate someone's free will, if someone else asks him to? Isn't that a bit problematic for God? What happens when the farmers ask for rain and the holidaymakers ask for sunshine?"

"Now you're pettifogging."

There is a small group of words that are the lexical equivalent of a young boy dressing up in his father's suit, or a girl wearing her mother's high-heeled shoes. The harder they try to act grown-up, the more ludicrous they become. "Pettifogging" belongs to this select group. At any rate, that's the way the word had struck both Yvette and John when they had encountered it in a novel shortly after they had met, and it had subsequently taken on the nature of a private joke between them.

"No I'm not," said John, trying hard not to smile. "I'm being deadly serious. During the Second World War, an attempt to assassinate Hitler came very close to succeeding. Unfortunately, it didn't and the plotters were executed. If they had succeeded, millions of lives could have been saved. Why did God choose to answer the prayers of Hitler's supporters instead of those who wanted to put a stop to his murderous regime?"

"I can't answer that question. But I have faith that God did what was right."

"How can it possibly be 'right' to allow a despotic regime to gas millions of its own citizens to death? Especially when the means of putting a stop to it was available, and needed only a minimum of intervention on God's part?"

"You can always find individual cases, where it is difficult for us to understand why God has acted in the way he has. Perhaps it is the problem that you yourself pointed out: a conflict of interests that cannot be resolved without violating someone's free will. It is not our place to question God's motives."

"Ours not to reason why, ours but to do and die?"

"Ours but to live and rejoice."

"So you are quite happy to rejoice in serving a God who refused to lift a finger to prevent a ruthless tyrant form murdering innocent men, women and children?"

"Oh John, you mustn't speak that way about God."

"Mustn't I? If a human being had been in a position to prevent the Nazi annihilation campaign, and had not lifted a finger to do so, he would have been put on trial at Nuremburg. Why should we judge God more leniently? Disposing of a vegetarian tyrant would have been a simple matter for someone who can magic a whole universe out of the void, impregnate virgins with his embryonic self, and raise corpses from the dead."

Keeping a fast-moving car on the packed snow of a winding country road is not a task that provides the driver with a lot of leisure time for admiring the view—either the magnificence of the scenery outside the car, or the pulchritude of passengers within. But the sound of a sob, coming from somewhere to the right of him, caused John to take his eyes off the road for long enough to cast a quick look at Yvette. There were tears in her eyes.

"John, please stop."

"I'm sorry if I have offended you. Dearest Yvette, I would rather be dead that harm a single hair on your lovely head. I'm not trying to hurt you, but to prevent you from throwing your life away in the service of a God who is not worthy of you."

"You don't understand, John. I'm not crying for my sake. I'm crying for your sake. You have invoked God's wrath."

"What right does God have to be angry with me?"

"What right do you have to question God's right?"

"Suppose that someone were to construct a robot, and that the robot dropped something valuable it was carrying and broke it. Would the robot's constructor have any right to be angry with the robot?"

"Whether or not he had any right to do so, it would be a futile thing for him to do."

"Then what makes it any less futile if God gets angry at us for things that we do? Assuming, of course, that he has created us."

"God has given us free will. We can be first-cause agents. That means that we must take responsibility for the things we decide to do."

"Suppose that in the—perhaps not too distant—future we are able to construct robots that can relieve hospital staff of tedious chores such as changing bed pans, turning bed-ridden patients, delivering meals, etc, freeing the human staff to spend more time tending to the personal welfare of their patients. Such a robot would need to have quite a lot of independent decision-making ability. Now let us suppose that one of these robots—which was being employed entirely in accordance with the manufacturer's instructions—happened to turn a patient over a bit carelessly and broke his back in the process. Who would be ultimately responsible—the robot or its manufacturer?"

"I don't believe that we will ever have robots which we can entrust to make life-or-death decisions about human beings."

"We already do."

"Where?"

"Ships and aircraft have auto-pilots. If the autopilot of an airliner made a wrong decision, it could send hundreds of people to their deaths. However, whether robots such as the ones I have described ever exist or not doesn't matter. It is highly unlikely that a tortoise and a hare would ever decide to have a race. Yet that doesn't prevent us from using them in Zeno's famous thought experiment. So what is your answer? Where would the responsibility lie: with the robot or its manufacturer?"

"With the manufacturer, I suppose."

"You sound as though there were room for doubt."

"No doubt as to where the responsibility would lie. But doubt about your scenario."

"Then you would not be prepared to let the manufacturer escape responsibility by claiming that he had equipped the robot with its own decision-making capability, and therefore the blame lay with the robot?"

"No. But if you mean that the robot's 'decision-making capability' is comparable to our free will, I don't accept that."

"Why not?"

"The robot can only do what we have equipped it to do. But God has put no restrictions on our free will."

"Hasn't he? Then why can't I fly? Why do I forget things that I have once known? Why can't I see God and his angels? Why am I in love with you instead of a Siamese cat? I am in every respect limited to doing only what God has equipped me to do—assuming, as we are, that it is God who has created me."

It would have been interesting to have heard Yvette's response. But, unfortunately, the author failed to make allowances for the increase of speed during the time Yvette's hand rested on John's arm, with the result that they arrived back at the cottage at precisely this juncture, to find Helen's car parked at the top of the drive. This made it necessary for our two theologians to devote their full attention to the task of manoeuvring their car down Yvette's toboggan slope to the house.

# Chapter 11

## Christmas Presents

Frosty, the Snowman, greeted John and Yvette as they opened the door to the cottage.

*... he was made of snow but the children know*
*how he came to life one day ...*

Someone had put the stack of Christmas records on the gramophone. The next thing to greet them was the smell of good cooking and the sight of people setting the table. If their attention had not been diverted, they might also have noticed some new packages under the Christmas tree, which were not there when they left. But it was diverted.

"Hullo, Yvette. You're as ravishing as ever! I don't see how you ever find the time to get any studying done. It must be a full-time job fending off all the males who want to take you out." Helen had always felt that John had been a nincompoop to ditch Yvette the way he did, and she hadn't hesitated to tell him so.

"Yvette has come up with a foolproof solution," said John, as Helen and Yvette hugged each other. "She's going to lock herself away where no man is allowed to enter."

"I've heard all about that. I can't say that I blame you, Yvette. Men are a pretty rotten lot on the whole. Just look at the way my brother treated you! But of course, there are exceptions, and I would like you to meet one of them. Yvette, this is my husband, Charles. Charles, this is Yvette."

During the five years since Helen had last seen Yvette, she had completed her teacher training, begun to work as a school teacher, met and married her husband, Charles, a newly-qualified doctor, and given birth to their first child, Kenneth, who was now 2 months old and sound asleep in the old white cot with removable sides that each of the Cunningham children had slept in when they were infants.

Charles was a tall slim man with a friendly smile, who looked more than capable of handling his wife's exuberance. "Hullo, Yvette. My wife has told me all about you. And for once she hasn't been exaggerating, at any rate not where looks are concerned. It remains to be seen whether you can do a triple backwards somersault on the back of a galloping horse, and all the other things that Helen claims you are capable of. But I have no doubt that you will prove her right there as well."

"Hullo, Charles. I'm pleased to meet you, and sorry to have to disappoint you. I wouldn't know how to sit on a horse, much less do somersaults on one."

"How was the service?" asked Sarah.

"Uplifting," replied Yvette. "St Luc-du-Lac is a wonderful monastery."

"And what did the music connoisseur make of it?" asked Andrew.

"I agree with Yvette." said John. "It's the right place to go to listen to Gregorian chant, and this was a choral service, so there was more singing and less of the monotone question-and-answer routine."

"Is there any reason why this conversation has to be held standing up in the hall?" asked Mrs Cunningham. "There's mulled wine, sandwiches and comfortable chairs waiting for you by the fire. If you don't get started now, it will be midnight before we have our dinner."

More out of, than in, step with the rollicking strains of "Ding Dong, Merrily on High," the little troupe marched over to the fireplace and drew up their chairs around the plate of sandwiches.

"The smelly ones are for you, Yvette," said Helen.

"Goodness, am I the only one who likes Oka cheese?" asked Yvette.

"You're the only one who's allowed to eat those sandwiches," replied Helen. "Mother says there was only half a cheese left, after someone polished off the other half yesterday, so it's FHB today."

(For the benefit of any reader who might have grown up in a family with unlimited resources, let it be explained that FHB means Family Hold Back, a command issued by the hostess when there is not enough of the expensive stuff to go around, telling family members to fill up on potatoes and go easy on the meat.)

"Lies! Humbug! Calumny!" retorted Mrs Cunningham. "Don't you believe a word of it, Yvette. There's plenty more of everything. I'm afraid that despite my best efforts, I have been unsuccessful in teaching my daughter the meaning of 'Thou shalt not bear false witness'. "

"Thank you for telling me, Mrs Cunningham. Otherwise I might have believed those lavish compliments Helen heaped on me when we arrived and become swollen-headed!" This time there was no question about it. That mischievous glint was definitely back.

After the sandwiches had made a second circuit and the wine glasses had been refilled, Mrs Cunningham announced "It's high time to hand out the presents. Since your father isn't here, John, you can officiate."

It was no small honour that his mother had bestowed upon John. In the Cunningham family it had always been Mr Cunningham's role to sit down beside the Christmas tree and hand out the presents. This was a task requiring logistic talent, good humour, and a thorough understanding of human psychology. If for any reason one person had fewer presents under the tree than other people, it was important to space them out, so that he or she was not left to watch everyone else opening their presents. It was also important not to hand out the best presents first, so that everything after that felt like an anti-climax.

It helped, of course, if as a child you had honed your recognition skills by squeezing and shaking the presents you received before opening them.

That there were presents under the tree at all, midway between Christmas and New Year's Eve, was because Helen's family had spent Christmas this year with Charles's parents in New Brunswick, so it was mostly presents for, and from, them that John had been asked to hand out.

He began by turning over the stack of Christmas records, putting "God Rest Ye Merry Gentlemen" on the bottom, so that it would be played first. This resulted in a good-natured cacophony as six voices tried to indicate, through phrasing and emphasis, where they thought the comma should be placed. Charles showed himself a worthy new member of this boisterous family by employing Victor Borge's ingenious phonetic pronunciation scheme to insert, not only commas, but semi-colons, exclamation marks and full stops at appropriate places.

The mathematically gifted reader may have wondered why there were not seven voices in the chorus. The reason is that John did not take part. We alluded above to the importance of psychological skills when carrying out the task with which he had been entrusted. John used the respite provided by the choral diversion to assess the job in front of him. By the time "We Wish You a Merry Christmas" had dropped down on top of "God Rest Ye Merry Gentlemen", he was ready.

He had decided to begin with the presents from Aunt Jennifer, a much-loved, and highly eccentric, unmarried sister of Mr Cunningham's. Aunt Jennifer put a lot of thought into her presents. They were never expensive, but always unusual—something that had not always been appreciated by her sister-in-law. For instance, the time she gave Andrew a ball that would stick to the wall you threw it at. Unfortunately, it would also stick—tenaciously—to the hair you threw it at, with the result that poor Sarah had spent a winter with the shortest haircut of any girl in her school.

This year it had been Mrs Cunningham's turn to host Christmas diner for the clan, so Aunt Jennifer had spent Christmas with them at the cottage. When you added in all the cousins, uncles, and aunts, there had been seventeen mouths for the 24-pound turkey to feed.

Aunt Jennifer had opted for hand puppets this year. Seventeen of them. John's had been a black-and-white cow, Mr Cunningham had received a lion, and his wife a tiger, or possibly a tigress—the puppet did not extend to the part of its anatomy that would have allowed this distinction to be made. In addition, there had been dogs, frogs, alligators, and Ali Baba, to name but a few.

Aunt Jennifer had led them in a rousing rendition of "Old MacDonald Had a Farm", in which she pointed at each puppet in turn to make suitable sounds in the appropriate places.

*Old MacDonald had a farm*
*E-I-E-I-O.*
*with a quack-quack [bow-wow, moo-moo, etc] here,*
*and a quack-quack there,*
*here a quack, there a quack, everywhere a quack-quack*
*Old MacDonald had a farm*
*E-I-E-I-O.*

Aunt Jennifer loved to sing. Her passion in life was opera, and she was actually quite a good singer, although John remembered mostly being embarrassed to stand beside her in church, where her voice could be heard above everyone else's during the singing of hymns.

Having heard that Yvette would be coming to the cottage in a few days, she had, on her return to Montreal, sent them a present for Yvette, which was now under the tree along with those for Helen, Charles and Kenneth.

However, before John could hand out these four new hand puppets—for that is what his investigations had led him to conclude they were—Kenneth announced that he was hungry. Or perhaps he just wanted to join in the merrymaking. His expression of utter contentment, once he had been attached to his mother's breast, lent credence to the former theory.

"A horse," exclaimed Charles, after tearing off the paper. He had forgotten that in the Cunningham household wrappings are removed carefully and folded up for reuse next year. But then he had come from a small family, where such frugality was not as important. And they weren't Scottish.

"It's not a horse, it's a camel, silly!" said Sarah.

"Does anyone know what sound a camel makes?" asked Mrs Cunningham, always the practical mother. "I think it had better be a horse, in case it has to sing 'Old MacDonald Had a Farm'."

At this point all eyes swung towards Yvette, who had begun to sing—in French. What they saw was a bald monk, wearing a brown vestment, on her right hand. They were singing alternate lines of a tune, which is *not* one of the canonical songs of the Catholic Church, although it is often sung as a canon.

*Sonnez les matines!*
Sonnez les matines!
*Din, dan, don.*
Din, dan, don.

"What have you got there, Yvette?" asked Mrs Cunningham.

"Frère Jacques, I think. Wasn't it thoughtful of Aunt Jennifer to give me something that I can bring with me to the convent! I'm sure the other nuns will enjoy having him around."

This time even John thought he could hear God laughing in the background.

"Yvette, can you hold Kenneth while I open my presents?" asked Helen, passing her son over to Yvette— and Frère Jacques, who was still on her hand.

In fairness to John, the chronicler feels obliged to point out that this was *not* something John had prearranged with Helen. However, the effect could not have been greater if he had. Suddenly an attractive young woman, who had decided to forego motherhood for the rest of her life, found herself with a newly-fed infant in her arms. Nor was Yvette at a loss, when Kenneth's contented gurgles turned into cries of discomfort. She put him on her shoulder and juggled him up and down until he let loose a burp that any two-month-old would have been proud of. And any mother.

Whilst this was going on, Helen opened her present from Aunt Jennifer, which looked as though it might be Winnie the Pooh, and John handed out the other presents to and from Helen's family. Then, holding the last present in his hands, he said, "Yvette, Helen didn't say you could keep Kenneth. He's only on loan."

Slightly flushed, Yvette handed Kenneth, who by this time was sound asleep, back to his mother.

"Thank you, Yvette. I couldn't have done it better myself!"

"Yvette, here's another thing, that we hope you will be able to take with you. It's from all the family."

"For me? But I haven't brought any presents for you. I didn't know that I was coming to celebrate Christmas!"

"That's no excuse, Yvette. You'll just have to make up for it by playing the piano for us after dinner," said Charles.

Yvette had spent enough time with the Cunninghams to know the routine. She opened her present carefully without tearing the wrapping paper. What she found inside was a photograph of her and all the Cunninghams, taken on the ski hill, on a sunny day about 6 years ago. It bore the simple inscription "To Yvette, with love from all of us." and it had been signed by everyone.

Yvette didn't try to hold back the tears, as she said "Thank you."

"Well then, that's that," said Mrs Cunningham. "John, you can be in charge of the toaster. We're having smoked salmon for starters, and then Turkey à la King for the main course. Helen and Charles have brought some fiddleheads with them from New Brunswick, which we'll have with the turkey.

# Chapter 12

## *Dinner with Helen's Family*

There may be readers who have not yet encountered the delicacy that takes is name from its resemblance to the scroll of a violin. Fiddleheads are baby ferns, picked in early spring before they have started to unfurl. Although they are at their best when steamed fresh, lightly salted and served with butter, they can be preserved in various ways, one of which is freezing. The most important thing to know about fiddleheads, however, is that they are delicious.

New Brunswick is world famous throughout the whole of New Brunswick as the home of fiddlehead cuisine. Charles's mother had sent some of her frozen fiddleheads with her son and daughter-in-law when they drove up from Fredericton. They had managed to keep them frozen on the roof rack of their car for the whole trip, and these tender greens were now waiting to be steamed for the main course.

"Bon appétit, everyone." With these words Mrs Cunningham gave the signal for the knife-and-fork orchestra to play the opening bars of the Smoked Salmon Overture.

"It would have been interesting to eavesdrop on the conversations that John and Yvette have been having," said Helen. "The Doubter and the Nun—it sounds like the title of a novel!"

"John is no longer a doubter," said Yvette.

It was as if the conductor had held up his hand. The orchestra stopped playing.

"Do you mean that you have managed to talk some sense into him?" asked a surprised Mrs Cunningham.

"No, that's not what I mean," replied Yvette dryly. "I mean that John is no longer in any doubt. He is quite certain that God does not exist."

"And what do you have to say in your defence, before we tie you to the stake?" asked Charles. "Are you guilty as charged? Do you wish to recant and place yourself at the mercy of the court?"

"Yvette's assessment is accurate," admitted John. "It is not something that I usually make an issue of. My position has been that the Christian moral code and sense of community is a common good worth preserving, even at the cost of accepting a God I don't believe in. However, Yvette's decision to devote herself exclusively to the service of that God, locked away in a place where she will be inaccessible to the entreaties of heartsick suitors ..."

"Whose names begins with 'J' and end in 'Cunningham', "interspersed Sarah.

"... has forced my hand."

"What has caused my dear brother to cross the Rubicon from agnosticism to atheism?" asked Helen.

"If you want to record all the gory details, you'll have to write that novel. However, the precipitating factor was a three-letter word."

"Not G-O-D, I take it?"

"No. W-H-Y."

"Why, 'why'?"

"It wasn't until one day, when I asked myself 'Why?', that I suddenly realized how preposterous the whole charade is. *Why* did God create us? *Why* would an almighty God, who could create anything he wanted to, as often as he wanted to, and give his creatures any qualities he wanted to, decide to create pathetic two-legged beings, whose mental capacity was so inferior to his own, that it makes as much sense to talk of love between him and us, as for me to talk of my love for an amoeba? *Why* would he deliberately create creatures that he knew would disobey him, when he was perfectly capable of creating creatures who would follow his commandments, as he demonstrated with Jesus? *Why* would he create smallpox, polio, cancer and other delights with which to inflict suffering and death upon his creation? *Why* would he do all this only once? And *why* would he keep himself hidden away from his creation?

"Did you get any answer?" asked Andrew.

"The only answer that I could come up with is that he created us to play with. We are his toys."

"Perhaps that novel should be called *God's Tin Soldiers*." suggested Andrew.

"If God exists, he must be sitting up there in his heaven, watching us murder one another, and die of cancer, the way we would watch a puppet show. Of course, I can't entirely rule out that this is exactly what he is doing. But I am not prepared to worship such a God. Nor, using the brain with which he has purportedly equipped me, am I prepared to believe that he exists."

"Poor Yvette. Is this what you have had to listen to for the past two days?" asked Mrs Cunningham.

"Basically, yes," replied Yvette, calmly.

"You must be a saint, to put up with it!"

"John has thought seriously, and honestly, about the same things that I have. Our starting points have been the same. It's just that we have come to different conclusions."

"Quite a difference!" exclaimed Sarah. "On the one hand a God of love. On the other a monster, indifferent to the sufferings of his creation."

"The decisive difference between John and me, is that he expects to be able to understand God logically, whereas I believe that God can only be understood through faith. It doesn't really matter what John, or anybody else— including myself—*thinks*. There is a reality out there. Either God exists, in which case whether or not we can

understand *why* he created us is irrelevant, or else God does
not exist, in which case the question is also irrelevant."

"Well put, Yvette!" said Mrs Cunningham with a
smile. "We could do with more people like you outside
convent walls. Perhaps you could serve God better from
within the community?"

"Well put, Mother!" said John. "She has already given
me better explanations of several doctrinal matters than I
have received from ordained ministers." John turned his
gaze upwards. "God, are you listening? We have taken a
vote down here, and would like you to send your servant to
us as our spiritual advisor, instead of keeping her locked
away in a cell with Frère Jacques."

Except for the time discrepancy, it would be easy to
believe that Leonardo da Vinci had been inspired by the
expression on Yvette's face to paint his masterpiece, the
*Mona Lisa*. With the same reservation, she might even have
served as an artist's model for the original Sphinx.

"I think I'm going to request a different seat at this
table." said Helen, who had been placed next to John. "Just
in case God decides to strike my irreverend brother with a
lightening bolt."

"Better than that, you can leave the table altogether,
and take the salmon plates with you," said Mrs
Cunningham. It's time for the main course. Andrew can
scrape off the dishes and stack them in the sink. Sarah, you
can help me carry in the food. John, you can serve the Pinot
Noir. We'll have to hope that the Almighty has not shown
his displeasure by turning it into water. Yvette and Charles
are excused from kitchen duties this time."

Before carrying out his mother's orders, John went over
to the gramophone and put the needle down on the top
record, which happened to be "Deck the Halls". Helen's
powerful contralto picked up the tune from the dining
room. She was joined almost immediately by Charles's

bass, and shortly thereafter by two sopranos and a baritone from the kitchen. Yvette, being a bit uncertain of the words, hummed along during the verses, but her mezzo joined in high-spiritedly on the "fa-la-las". Although John had sung tenor in the choir, the setting was too high to be pleasurable, so he joined Charles singing bass-baritone. If Walt Disney had been able to observe the to-ings and fro-ings under the Cunningham roof on this winter's evening, the Seven Dwarfs might today be remembered for singing whilst they worked, instead of whistling.

"Isn't it strange, that John likes Christmas so much!" exclaimed Sarah, after everybody had tasted, and complemented Mrs Cunningham on, the delicious food she had put before them.

"Yes—considering that he doesn't believe in Christ," agreed Helen, who couldn't have been too worried about lightning bolts, since she had retained her place beside John at the table.

"But I *do* believe in Christmas," replied John. "I don't believe in God, but I believe in love. Christmas is a time of love. Christmas has very little to do with God. There were mid-winter celebrations all over the world before Christianity came along and took them over. In England it was called *Yule*. In the Scandinavian countries it is still called *Jul*. My guess is that these are Yule logs embroidered on the table cloth."

"*Hark the herald angels sing, glory to the new-born King*," sang Sarah in her clear soprano voice. "Who do you envisage as the King, when you sing that song?"

"*Jingle bells, jingle bells, jingle all the way*," replied John in a light baritone. "*Deck the halls with boughs of holly*. Where's the King? *I'm dreaming of a white Christmas*. Some of our best-loved Christmas carols are written by non-Christians."

"Surely it's a bit preposterous of you to claim that Christmas has little to do with God, John," said Mrs Cunningham firmly. "It's Jesus' birthday—the mass of Christ!"

"Do you think that was uppermost in Aunt Jennifer's mind when she bought us those hand puppets? Is that what you were thinking about when you cooked this delicious Christmas dinner?" asked John. "How many people think about God, when they put the decorations on their Christmas trees? How many children associate Father Christmas, or Santa Claus, with Christ? Father Christmas is a vehicle through whom we channel our love for one another. We don't buy presents as a tribute to God—or to enrich the merchants who sell them—but to see the faces of our children, friends and relatives light up when they tear off the wrappings. Or fold them up, as the case may be.

"All over the world at this time of year, in hundreds of millions of homes, people gather together to exchange gifts, sing songs and put aside their petty differences in a gigantic outpouring of love. They do so not because any God has commanded them to do so, or threatened to throw them into hell fires if thy do not, but because they have chosen to."

"So, you believe in the religion of Christmas?" suggested Andrew.

"There's more wisdom in that question, than you perhaps realize," replied John. "It seems to me that a new religion is being born before our very eyes. The similarity with other major religions is striking: at the centre of them all is an invisible father figure, who keeps track of whether we've been good or bad, and rewards us accordingly. An important difference is that Father Christmas rewards us in this life, if we've been good, and if we've misbehaved, the punishment is to go without presents, a considerable improvement on being thrown into hell fires!

"At the same time that we see church attendance diminishing, we see the celebration of Christmas playing an increasingly important role in our lives. And I'm all in favour of it. Whereas the priests of the revealed religions tell us that we have been created by their respective Supreme Beings, and that we must obey an obscure set of rules which only they can interpret, Father Christmas has been created by us, and there is no possibility of any high priest telling us that He has commanded us to commit atrocities in His name. Surely that is something worth building on?"

"But is there any reason why Christmas can't be all this, and at the same time be a celebration of the God of love?" asked Mrs Cunningham.

"I used to ask myself the same question," replied John. "Does it make any difference if we continue to believe in magic, as long as the emphasis continues to shift from burning heretics to loving our neighbours? Can't we just be patient and let the Christian God travel the same path already trodden by the various sun gods, and the Egyptian, Greek, Roman, and Norse gods before it?"

"You sound as if the answer is 'no'," said Andrew.

"I fear that we can't afford that luxury."

"Why not?"

"If Christianity were the only religion in town, we could," replied John. "But it's not. Some of the poorest, most densely populated countries in the world have large Muslim populations. As these populations continue to expand, they are not going to meekly jostle for standing room in their overcrowded homelands, whilst their television programs show them well-fed infidels in sparsely-populated countryside wallowing in the lap of luxury. Their holy book, the Koran, tells them in no uncertain terms that they must not rest until the entire world has been conquered for Islam. It also warns them not to befriend Christians or Jews, and explicitly tells them that Jesus was *not* the son of God.

Since it is a dogma of Muslim faith that every word in the Koran has been dictated by God himself, this is non-negotiable. Islam is totally incompatible with Christianity, and if we insist on clinging to our beliefs in our respective Gods, this will inevitably lead to global conflicts that will make religious wars of the past look like Sunday-school picnics."

"What a dreary picture. Yvette, you must be looking forward to getting away from all this," said Helen.

"I must confess, that the thought had crossed my mind," confessed Yvette.

"If I didn't have other commitments, I'd be tempted to join you!" exclaimed Helen.

"Well, you all have other commitments," announced Mrs Cunningham. "Dessert is lemon meringue pie. It will take about 15 minutes in the oven. John, you can make the coffee. I suggest the rest of you get started on the washing up, so that there won't be so much to do afterwards."

Once again, Walt Disney would have been interested to watch these seven revellers at work, as they sang *O Come All Ye Faithful*, closely followed by *I Saw Mummy Kissing Santa Claus*.

One of the places where the Cunningham's Scottish heritage shone through, was in their choice of liqueur. If guests insisted on it, which French ones frequently did, good-quality Cognac could be produced—although Mr Cunningham insisted on calling it brandy. There was even a "top ten" assortment of other liqueurs occupying a shelf in the liquor cabinet. But pride of place was taken by a whisky liqueur from the Isle of Skye.

It was this, which Mrs Cunningham offered her guests with their coffee, adding as an afterthought, "or would you like something else?" Knowing that this potation was almost as important a part of a Cunningham Christmas as plum pudding, no one opted for something else. However, Kenneth's milk producer asked for "just a few drops".

"One friar and one framed photograph: that must be worth at least two Christmas carols of our choosing," said Charles. "I opt for *Lo, How a Rose E'er Blooming* and *White Christmas.*"

"There's been enough ungodly talk, this evening," said Sarah. "Let's sing some traditional carols and put Christ back into Christmas. How about *Away in a Manger* and *It Came Upon the Midnight Clear.*"

"I second Sarah's motion," said Mrs Cunningham. "But Yvette doesn't get off that lightly. First she has to help the rest of you clear off the table and finish washing the dishes."

Seldom have 7 people worked together in such jollity. And seldom have bone china and crystal glasses been handled with such abandon. It was not without a sense of relief, that Mrs Cunningham put the last unscathed liqueur glass back on the shelf, and closed the door of the china cabinet.

Yvette did not play dispassionately. She had been heartened by Sarah and Mrs Cunningham's repertoire suggestions, and put her heart into her playing. And everyone else put their hearts into their singing. Including John. Any dust which might have remained on the cottage rafters after last night's songfest, got thoroughly shaken off tonight.

"I hope that you feel sufficiently recompensed for the wonderful presents you have given me," said Yvette, at last. "I suggest we finish with a song for John, who has been such a good sport and sung about Christ and God without flinching."

It would be unjust of the chronicler to suggest that the gleam in Yvette's eyes was in any way related to *schadenfreude*. That worthy maiden would not have allowed herself to harbour such an uncharitable emotion. By candlelight it was difficult to make an accurate assessment. However, the gleam spoke of something more than the mere mischievousness that we have encountered on a number of previous occasions.

"John, this is for you," said Yvette, turning towards him. "But the words are to be interpreted with the same abstraction that you have applied to the previous carols in praise of God." With that, Yvette broke into a rousing rendition of *Let it snow! Let it snow! Let it snow!* Everyone joined in with gusto, especially in the last verse.

> *The fire is slowly dying*
> *and my dear, we're still goodbying,*
> *but as long as you love me so,*
> *let it snow! let it snow! let it snow!*

Yvette finished with a two-handed glissando, jumped up and pecked John on the cheek. To a ringing round of applause.

# *Chapter 13*

## *A Last Walk Under the Stars*

Much has been written about those joyous events which cause us for the first time suddenly to hear the birds singing, or notice the fragrance of the flowers, or delight in the white, ever-changing sculptures drifting across the blue sky overhead—despite the fact that we have walked along the same path hundreds of times before without being aware of these things. Far less has been written about the opposite events, which silence the birds, stifle the fragrances, and make us uninterested in celestial art galleries. The events of this evening have given the chronicler an opportunity to redress that imbalance.

Nature's splendour had not changed since the previous occasion, twenty-four hours ago, when Ron had taken John and Yvette out for a stroll in the cold night air. Tonight the same stars glistened in the same black dome above the same threesome. The snow which crunched under their feet was indistinguishable from that of the previous evening. Admittedly, the snow banks at the side of the road were a bit higher, making it harder for Ron to reach the trees, but this minor discrepancy could not account for the totally altered way in which John reacted to the spectacle which engulfed them.

Last night he had been filled with the ecstasy of falling in love again. Tonight he had to face up to the fact that his love was unrequited. What was the use of a heaven full of stars, when the girl he loved had spurned him? The crunching of snow only made him feel that it was his own emotions being trampled under foot.

Andrew had suggested that Ron understood what was going on in the minds of his humans a lot of the time. Tonight seemed to be one of those times. As our threesome made its way between the snow banks, beneath the canopy of stars, Ron never ventured far from Yvette. If he was obliged to leave her briefly, in order to spray a few drops of his own scent over that left by some canine trespasser, he soon returned to her side. It was as if he sensed that this was the last walk they would ever have together.

"Will I be invited to the wedding?" asked John.

"I'm afraid not," laughed Yvette. "It's a religious ceremony, for nuns only. Besides, becoming the Bride of Christ must be sheer nonsense to an evolutionary biologist, who only believes in things he can put his hand on or see in his microscope."

"Don't be too hard on us. Even if we probably won't be able to help you, we may be able to help future generations of nuns to a more physically satisfying relationship with their husband."

"Oh?"

"Today we can grow complete new plants from a very small piece of a parent plant. In fact, it is not uncommon for all of the potato plants in a farmer's field to be clones of the same plant. Every cell of a living being, with the exception of sex cells, contains all the information needed to produce a complete individual. It is stored in the cell's DNA. It's only a matter of time before we will be able to grow humans and other animals from the DNA in a single cell. After all, that is what a fertilized egg does."

"So?"

"Well, suppose that an archaeologist were to find some relic of Jesus. His mother might have done what many mothers do, and saved one of his milk teeth, or a lock of his hair, for example. It would then be possible to create a new Jesus—the Second Coming, perhaps?

"In fact, it would be possible to do better than that. If we only produced one new Jesus, he would have a hard job satisfying all of his brides. But there would be no reason to stop at one. In the womb it is not uncommon for a fertilized egg to split in two, producing identical twins. Once we are able to grow embryos from DNA and nurture them in artificial wombs, we would be able to produce enough identical Jesuses to provide each nun with her own.

"That would, of course, require that each Jesus was willing to marry the nun to whom he had been assigned, a problem for which biologists may not be able to come up with a solution. It would also pose a problem for theologians. The term *Trinity* would no longer be adequate to describe a godhead with a multitude of members. The *Multiplicity*, perhaps?

"Who knows, perhaps this would eventually lead to a new race of sinless humans and God would be able to extinguish the fires of hell for good. It would certainly save on his energy bill—even if it made his life a lot duller."

"Do you really believe the nonsense you're spouting, or are you just trying to provoke a reaction from me?"

If John's intention had been the latter, he had failed. By starlight, and at a gentlemanly distance, it was impossible for John to tell whether Yvette's eyes, barely discernable beneath her fur cap, contained that tell-tale glint of amusement. But her voice contained the vocal equivalent.

"I guess, if I am to be completely honest—which I try hard to be, despite my non-belief in God—my reason for saying it *was* to provoke some sort of reaction. When you get bogged down with a difficult problem, and seem to be going around in circles, sometimes the best way to make progress is to throw in a new idea—however preposterous it may be—and see if your reaction to it doesn't provide you with a new path to explore. However, the scenario I have hinted at—even if highly improbable—cannot be ruled out entirely."

"So I'm the problem you feel bogged down with?"

"Not you as a person. Far from regarding you as a problem, I can think of no happier fate than to spend the rest of my life with you at my side. But your decision to make that impossible by shutting yourself away from the world in a nunnery *is* a problem which has me completely bogged down, and we have been going around in circles ever since we got here."

"Has it occurred to you that what you consider to be an intractable 'problem', involves my right to make up my own mind?"

"Yes, it has occurred to me. So often that it has etched itself upon my consciousness—in large capital letters. All I can say in my defence is that I do not in any way question your right to make up your own mind. However, I hope you will grant me the right to try to influence your decision. Your decision does, after all, affect me. It affects me deeply."

Yvette's voice softened. "I know. That's why I have put up with all the blasphemous things you have been saying. I do grant you the right to try and influence my decision. But I'm afraid the time is fast approaching when you will have to accept 'no' for an answer."

"Before I do, a hypothetical question. Suppose that we had both been born a thousand years from now, and I was a recreated Jesus. Would you marry me?"

Yvette laughed. She laughed in the whole-hearted, unaffected way that so endeared her to John—and apparently without a thought for the scorecard on which God was appraising her fitness for nunship.

"I don't know about marrying you. But I would like to have you as court jester."

"Now let's get this straight. You are prepared today to marry a man who will never be able to provide you with anything other than imaginary companionship; yet when offered the opportunity to have the real thing as a husband you turn him down? You even laugh at him!"

"But I wasn't laughing at the real Jesus. I was laughing at the real John Cunningham. The whole idea of someone who denies the very existence of God being a reincarnation of Christ is just too absurd to be taken seriously."

"Then we have at least established one thing."

"What's that?"

"Jesus was born without a free will."

"How does that follow?"

"If he had a free will, he would be just as capable as I am of rejecting God altogether, yet still proposing marriage to you, just as I have."

"I wasn't aware that you had proposed to me," replied Yvette, with a twinkle in her voice.

Blast it! Can't she see how much fun life would be together? John asked himself. So what, if God chuckled occasionally about the Garden of Eden. Could he hug her, kiss her, pull her pony tail, pay the bills, give her children?

"I haven't, formally. As I mentioned earlier, I believe that, to be successful, a marriage needs to be between two people who are equally committed to one another. Your commitment to me at this point appears to be less than zero. When a girl laughs at a boy's advances, I think it is safe to assume that her commitment is in negative territory. However, lest there be any doubt in your mind: please be aware that a change of heart on your part would lead to my becoming very formal."

"I don't think that I would like you, if you went all formal. The John I like is capable of saying the most outrageously informal things."

"Did I hear you say that you liked someone called John?"

"Yes. I value him as a friend. But I am not prepared to marry him."

"Not even if he were genetically identical to Jesus, apparently."

"You are overlooking a crucial factor."

"What is that?"

"It is conceivable that scientists in the future may be able to create living organisms from human DNA. But they will not be humans. They will not have a spirit, which comes from God—unless, of course God chooses to breath his spirit into them. It will be the *mechanism* of a human, an empty shell with no spiritual qualities, like a car without a driver."

"Hmm. Do pigs have a spirit?"

"No."

"What about monkeys?"

"No. Only man has been created in God's image. Only man possesses a divine spirit."

"What about Neanderthal Man?"

"I don't know."

"Australopithecus?

"I don't know, but I don't think so. I don't think they were created in God's image."

"So there's a line that goes somewhere, and we happen to be on the right side of it?"

"Is that a problem? Perhaps God was experimenting with his design, and it wasn't until he produced *Homo sapiens* that he felt satisfied. Perhaps he tried giving Neanderthals a spirit, but decided it wasn't good enough. I don't know, and I don't feel the need to know."

"Could it be that God is still experimenting, and will soon come up with something better? Perhaps a human who will finally obey God's laws, and put the Devil out of business? *Homo perfectus*? Perhaps biologists are part of God's plan. Perhaps he plans to use us to produce this new species of human from Jesus' DNA."

"You do have a fertile imagination, John!" laughed Yvette.

"Suppose that's what happens. Then the new humans would be able, without exerting themselves, to lead the sinless lives that we can't accomplish, no matter how hard we try. All our efforts would then appear as futile to *Homo perfectus* as those of the Neanderthals appear to us. Your life of devotion in a cold convent cell would be as significant to them as that of a Neanderthal woman in her cave is to us. At least, if you were to choose the alternative, you could have fun in the here and now."

"I assume that 'the alternative' you are referring to is yourself?"

"As a matter of fact, yes."

"What are you doing?" asked Yvette, as John fell into step close behind her.

"Weren't you about to instruct the devil to take up a position in the rear?"

"I didn't realize that you had become a mind reader. Can you juggle too?" asked Yvette, with what sounded like a smile in her voice.

"Now then, Mr Satan, let's suppose that your conjectures are *not* what happens. Then I would have turned down God's invitation in order to spend my life with an atheist, and we would both spend eternity in a very hot place."

"But you would probably get a reduction of sentence for good behaviour. And who knows, as Mother suggested at the dinner table, you might even be able to serve God better from outside convent walls, which would, if there's any justice in the World to Come, entitle you to spend eternity being serenaded by angels. The mere fact that you would be on hand in this world to cancel out any bad influence my ungodly remarks might have on our acquaintances would surely entitle you to a direct flight to Heaven."

"But have you stopped to consider what that would involve for me? How appealing do you suppose the prospect of having my faith challenged every day of my life by my own husband is to me? John, I would like to remember you as a good friend, with whom I have shared many happy moments, not as an enemy, who constantly attacked my faith."

It was as if the wind had dropped and left John's sails flapping lifelessly.

"Mother was right, Yvette. You have been a saint to put up with my repeated assaults on your faith. I hope you realize that I have been driven by love for you, not by any ill will towards your religion. Had you chosen to serve God in some other way, which did not involve locking yourself away from the world—and from me—it would not have been necessary."

"Would that have been better? I'm grateful that you made your position known from the outset. It would have been much worse if you had said nothing, and I had discovered too late that the man I had fallen back in love with was an atheist."

The two theologians and their canine companion had come to the end of their nocturnal perambulation. John shut the cottage door and hung Ron's leash on the hook behind it.

"Goodnight, John."

"Goodnight, Yvette."

# Chapter 14

## Breakfast, Cribbage and Lunch

Yvette had been right all along. There *was* a God. The proof was all around him. It was irrefutable. John was in Kingdom Come. Listening to heavenly music. He recognized the tune: Schubert's G-flat Impromptu. His favourite piano music. Why were the angels playing it on harps? Didn't God have a piano? Wait a minute, what was he doing in Heaven? Unbelievers, like him, get sent to the Other Place.

With the aid of the small trickle of brain cells that had begun reporting for duty, John gradually pieced together a more coherent picture. They weren't playing harps at all. It was someone playing a piano. And the sound was coming from somewhere beneath him, not from on high. And he wasn't in Heaven, he was in bed. In the cottage. The only person in the cottage who could play the piano like that was Yvette.

The music stopped, and so did John's limited thought processes.

"Good morning, sleepyhead!"

It was that attractive young lady again, with her mug of tea. This time she managed to put the tray down on the bedside table and withdraw out of reach before John succeeded in opening an eye and getting his brain into first gear.

"I hope you slept well?"

"How should I know, at this ungodly hour?"

"It's 9 o'clock."

"So you think that just because you brought me a cup of tea, you're entitled to wake me up in the middle of the night?"

"I promise not to do it again."

There it was! That was the thought that had been struggling in vain to get his attention ever since the first grey cells had begun to stir this morning. This was the last day! He would never see Yvette again. Is that why she had played Schubert this morning? Was it her way of saying goodbye—for ever?

John sat up and reached for the tea.

"Thank you. A cup of tea in the morning is worth more than a pot of gold."

"You're welcome. But I'm afraid you'll have to make it yourself tomorrow."

"Is there no way I can induce you to change your mind?"

"I had hoped that we were done with inducing."

John sighed, silently. "Yes, Yvette. You have withstood your 40 days in the wilderness and I hope that you will be richly rewarded. You deserve the cell with the best view."

"You seem to have forgotten. The views that are important to me are not the temporal ones that can be seen through a window."

"Well then, I wish you lots and lots of wonderful non-temporal views."

"They are not dependent upon the good wishes of any human." Then, realizing the unintended harshness of her words, she added, "But, thank you for your kind thoughts."

Tea has an invigorating effect on sleepy brain cells. John's brain was shifting into second gear. A thought struck him.

"Have you and God had a chuckle yet, this morning?"

"No. I have been giving thanks that my trial is nearing its end, and that I will soon be able to devote myself entirely to His service."

"Something has just occurred to me."

"Yes?"

"With so many brides, who gets to bring Jesus his tea in the morning?"

This caught Yvette off guard, and she laughed.

"You are incorrigible, John!"

"Will you promise me one thing?"

"That depends on what it is."

"Will you try to smuggle out a message, and let me know the answer?"

Yvette, who had just managed to straighten out her face, found the corners of her mouth turning involuntarily upwards again. "I'll let you know."

"It would also be interesting to know whether he takes milk and sugar."

Luckily, John had put down the tea mug. Otherwise one of his socks, which Yvette picked up and threw at him, might have caused an accident.

By the time he arrived at the breakfast table, everyone else had finished eating, and they were sitting around nursing their second or third cups of tea or coffee. Except for Kenneth, who was noisily gulping down his meal of Turkey à la King and lemon meringue pie, which his mother had reprocessed for him during the night, and was now dispensing from her attractive containers.

John did not have to endure any snide remarks about Rip van Winkle or Sleeping Beauty this morning. It was as if his siblings had reached an unspoken agreement to be kind to him on this day of sorrow. It may also have been because they themselves were feeling sad. They were all fond of Yvette, and would have liked to welcome her into the family.

"Do you remember how to play cribbage, Yvette?" asked Sarah.

Yvette was one of probably very few French Canadians who knew how to play this game, in which the score is kept by sticking matchsticks into holes in a wooden board. Rumour has it that the board first saw service as a device used by Neanderthals to keep track of how many meals they could get out of one mammoth.

Be that as it may, after some further development, the game of cribbage had taken root in the British Isles, and John's forebears had brought it with them from Scotland. Anyone would lead a lonely life in the Cunningham household, who looked the other way when the cribbage board was brought forth. Yvette had learned to play so well that she and John had been a winning team, holding their own against the best that Lake Gomareph could pit against them.

"I don't know. I haven't played for five years," replied Yvette.

"How about a game then, for old time's sake? Andrew and I challenge you and John. The winners can play Helen and Charles."

The most important thing about cribbage, as far as John was concerned, was that it was not bridge. You do not play cribbage in deadly earnest. You do not have to remember all the hands that have been played previously. There are no arcane signals, such as a bid of "2 diamonds", which really means "I have the Ace and Queen of spades, the King of Hearts, 3 face cards in clubs and I'll kick you under the table if you don't bid No Trump."

Cribbage, or 'crib' as it is affectionately known, is an excuse for sitting down with your friends. A complete hand seldom lasts more than a minute, after which you can forget about the cards that have just been played, and continue to joke, solve the world's problems, or scratch the dog behind his ears, whilst the cards are gathered in, shuffled and a new hand dealt.

"I'll drive around to the bakers and pick up some bread for lunch, while you're playing." announced Charles.

"I'll come with you. You can drop me off at Eileen's on the way, and pick me up on the way back," said Mrs Cunningham. "I want to straighten out a few things with her."

"If it's about Yvette," said John, "she has already promised to squelch Mrs Bigmouth's rumour."

"I'm glad to hear it. But I need a few things for the weekend anyway."

John had told himself that it was all over. Yvette deserved to have her decision respected. His task now was to fall out of love with her. He had told himself dozens of times. The trouble was that he couldn't bring himself to believe it. There she was, sitting across the table from him. Her slightest movement excited passion within him. She was everything he could possibly desire in a partner. And here he was, playing a game of crib with her, as if it was something they could do any day of the week—when instead he was going to drive her back to Montreal in a few hours, after which he would probably never see her again.

"Fifteen-two, fifteen-four, and a double run makes twelve," said Yvette.

"Fifteen-two, fifteen-four, and a double run *of four* makes fourteen," corrected Andrew.

"Oh, thank-you, Andrew. I forgot to count the turn-up," said Yvette with appreciation.

Cribbage aficionados will notice that Muggins' rule, which allows a player to claim any points missed by his opponent, was not being used in this game. Muggins' rule is optional, and must be agreed on by all players before the game begins. It was John's conviction that Muggins' rule had been invented by a jealous bridge player, determined to sabotage the camaraderie which exists around a cribbage table, and he refused to play with it. In this, he and Yvette had been in complete agreement.

The chronicler would like to intervene and point out that, although the other members of the Cunningham family shared John's enthusiasm for cribbage, they did not all share his views on bridge. His mother was an excellent, and his father a passable, bridge player. Mrs Cunningham had seen to it that all her children had learnt to play bridge, in the same way that Mr Cunningham had ensured that they all learned to play tennis, feeling that it was a social skill that would stand them in good stead later in life. She was a much sought-after bridge partner, and there is no question but that the game enriched her life.

"Sorry, John. I'm afraid I've let you down. I'm just too out of practice."

"The game's not over yet. They may be ahead, but we get to count first next time."

"Twenty-two for two", said Andrew, matching John's six, which followed Sarah's Jack. With this he moved their peg to the 120th hole. Just one more point and they would win.

"Twenty-eight for six!" said Yvette, playing another six and moving their front peg to eight points from the last hole.

"Thirty," said Sarah, putting down her last card, which was a two.

"Thirty-one for two," said John, playing the last card, an ace, which brought them six holes from the finish.

Yvette counted first. She had a four, a five, a six, and a Queen. Seven points.

"Congratulations!" said Sarah, and hugged Yvette. Andrew also gave Yvette a big hug.

"It's fine for you two," said John, "but if I tried that, I'd get a very different reaction!"

"Yvette gave you a kiss last night. We all saw it," said Sarah.

"That wasn't a kiss. It was a peck on the cheek. Anyway, a kiss that everybody sees doesn't count," said John, despondently.

Under different circumstances, one of his siblings would have been sure to say "cheer up". But they all realized that there was nothing for John to feel cheerful about, and they spared him this platitude.

"Yvette, Charles isn't back yet," said Helen. "Why don't we cancel our game, and you can take this victory with you to the cloister. I don't expect you will be playing any cribbage there?"

"That would be defeating the purpose of a cloister," replied Yvette. "The whole idea is to provide a retreat from the cares and trivia of the temporal world."

She sounded other-worldly enough when she said it. But John noticed something: there was colour in her cheeks. Yvette had enjoyed taking part in this heathen Anglo-Saxon rite, and it mattered to her that she and John had won. She had better hope that God was looking the other way.

"You have certainly had your share of temporal cares to cope with during the past couple of days!" said Sarah. "I can understand that you are looking forward to putting it all behind you."

"It's all part of God's plan. I shall remember the warmth I have experienced within your family with fondness, and it will serve me as a reminder of what Christian faith as the foundation for family life can accomplish—even if it is not Catholic."

"With one notable exception!" suggested Andrew.

"That has also been part of God's plan," said Yvette, as the colour left her cheeks. "My conversations with John will serve as a reminder to me of the folly of trying to understand God through logical thought. *Quisquis non receperit regnum Dei velut parvulus, non intrabit in illud.*"

"Something about God and small," said Sarah, whose high-school Latin was no match for Yvette's.

"Only by receiving the kingdom of God like a child, can you enter in."

John wondered whether someone who could quote passages from the Bible in Latin was really capable of entering into heaven, or anywhere else, as a child. And he wondered what had happened to his free will, if he was being manipulated as part of God's plan for Yvette. But he realized that it didn't matter any more. Nothing did.

"So for the rest of your life, you will remember me as a cautionary example," said John sadly.

"I will also remember the happy times we had together during our school years."

"What might have been—if I had not committed the sin of thinking for myself."

At this point Ron galloped in to announce that the shoppers had returned, and thoughts turned to lunch.

A question that has been hotly debated is what the most significant North American contribution to world cuisine has been. Suggestions that have been put forward—usually by foreigners—have included hamburgers, milk shakes, chocolate chip cookies and corn on the cob. But for someone who has actually grown up in North America, there can be no doubt. The answer is peanut butter.

When schoolchildren sit down to exchange sandwiches from their lunch boxes, the question they ask each other is not "What kind of sandwiches do you have?" but "What do you have on your peanut butter sandwiches?"

Peanut butter sandwiches contain hyphens: peanut-butter-and-jam, peanut-butter-and-honey, peanut-butter-and-banana, peanut-butter-and-bacon, peanut-butter-and-mayonnaise, to name but a few.

If placed end to end, the number of peanut-butter sandwiches consumed by the average North American by the time he or she graduates from high school might not quite stretch all the way around the equator, but it would almost certainly extend from home to school and back.

The secret to making good peanut-butter sandwiches is fresh bread.

This Charles now provided in abundance. Two large crusty loaves of still-warm bread were placed on separate breadboards. Peanut butter, jam, bananas, and all the other accoutrements were produced, and the kitchen was soon abuzz with knife-wielding evangelicals, offering to make the One True Peanut-Butter Sandwich for anyone willing to step forward and be converted.

After years of vacillation, John had finally allowed himself to be baptised into the Peanut-Butter-and-Lettuce sect. Yvette had at first treated peanut butter with the disdain of someone in whose ancestral language the menus of the world's leading restaurants are still written, considering peanut butter to be a plebeian Anglo-Saxon invention. But even she would condescend to eat—and even enjoy—peanut-butter sandwiches when the bread was still warm from the oven. When John offered to make her some with lettuce, she needed no further persuasion.

"Well, Yvette, it has been wonderful to see you again, and I hope that you will find your chosen vocation truly fulfilling," said Mrs Cunningham.

"Yes, so do we," said Sarah. "We'll miss you, but perhaps we'll be able to get together again some day."

"And sing some more Christmas carols!" added Helen.

"Do angels sing Christmas carols?" wondered Andrew.

"What makes you think that you'll be heading in that direction?" asked Charles. "Yvette, I'm very glad that I finally had a chance to meet you. Please put in a good word for us, when you get God's ear. Even if we seem a bit irreverent at times, we mean well. And we wish you all the best."

There were tears in Yvette's eyes, as she said "Thank you."

# Chapter 15

## The Drive Back to Montreal

There are a few pieces of classical piano music that can almost be enjoyed even when badly played by a rank amateur—especially if that amateur happens to be someone near and dear to you. The first movement of *Moonlight Sonata* and *Liebstraum No 3* (without the runs) fall into this category. But Liszt's *Hungarian Rhapsody No 2*, which Yvette and John were listening to on the car radio, does not.

Not that any rank amateur would even try. This fireworks display of piano virtuosity can only be pulled off by the very best pianists. Yvette might have been one of them, if she had continued with her piano studies, thought John, as he steered the car towards Montreal. But she had been called to what she felt was a more important task—and what John considered to be a waste of her life.

The sun was shining, the fields were white, the villages they drove through could have been sets for a Hollywood movie. All that was missing was the story with a happy ending.

There didn't seem to be much sense in starting a conversation. They had already talked about all the important things, and neither of them was in the mood to talk about trivial things. Instead, they listened together to the music they both loved.

John had long ago come to the conclusion that it was almost impossible to get anyone to change strongly held beliefs through logical argument. It had taken hundreds of years for the Catholic Church to finally accept that the Earth revolves around the Sun, an idea that Copernicus had put forward in 1530. The Church fathers insisted that the Earth was the centre of the universe, and therefore everything else must revolve around it. They were prepared to burn Galileo at the stake for supporting Copernicus.

There are probably people who still believe the world is flat. There are people who believe that they have been in contact with aliens. Many fundamentalists, whatever their religion, do not accept that humans are descended from apes.

John knew someone quite well who refused to believe in viruses. John had even shown him photographs of a virus taken with an electron microscope. But this had made no difference. It was just some concentration of molecules, probably part of the host organism, maintained the sceptic.

He himself had been impervious to arguments against a belief in God. It wasn't until he, on his own, had begun to find holes in the arguments put forward *in favour of* such a belief, that he had begun to loose faith. Perhaps strongly-held beliefs can only be changed from within. Unfortunately, there was no sign of any such change of thinking taking place inside the pretty head of his travelling companion.

Somewhat begrudgingly, John admitted to himself that he admired Yvette all the more for her strength of character. What did it matter that Joan of Arc may have been mistaken about where her voices came from? If she hadn't listened to them, she would not have changed the course of history, and the world would have been a drearier place. He would have to console himself that the rest of his own life would be less dreary, for his having known Yvette.

John carried Yvette's bag to her front door.

"Goodbye, Yvette. I wish you well in your chosen life. I shall miss you."

Yvette showed no sign of wanting to be hugged. He wondered whether he should shake her hand. But that seemed too contrived.

"John"

"Yes?"

"I had a long talk with God on the way back."

"How is he?"

"He has decided that I don't have enough detachment for a life of contemplation. He wants me to serve him from within society."

John's mouth was open, but no words issued forth.

"Perhaps you could give me a call after the weekend?"

"After the weekend? *After the weekend?* I'll give you a call tonight. I'll give you a call right now!" John pretended to hold a telephone receiver to his ear. "Hullo? Yvette? Would you like to go out for dinner with me tonight? Would you like to have dinner with me every night? For the rest of your life?"

"No, John," smiled Yvette. "I need a few days to adjust my thinking. But Monday would be nice.

"And, John"

"Yes?"

"I haven't promised anything. You're still an apostate, as far as I am concerned. But I might enjoy another game of crib."

# Chapter Notes

If you have reached this point, without once having been overcome by the compelling urge to look up some fact for yourself, it is suggested that you close the book now and consider it read. Some of the notes which follow are highly technical, and the titillation level of most of them is probably pretty close to zero.

As explained in the preface, these notes are provided for the benefit of those pitiable individuals who suffer from a compulsion to look everything up for themselves. (The author is thus afflicted.) There should be more than enough information on the following pages to satisfy even the most avid researcher.

Please see the preface for suggestions on using these notes.

The *Bible* quotations are from the Authorized (King James) Version, unless otherwise indicated.

## Preface

iii     "Ships that pass in the night ..."
        Henry Wadsworth Longfellow (1807-1882)
        *Tales of a Wayside Inn* (1863-1874) Part iii, The
        Theologian's Tale: Elizabeth, iv.

## Chapter 1 – The Drive From Montreal

5    "Lord Ronald, a six-year old golden retriever who
     had been so named after one of Stephen Leacock's
     characters"

> "Lord Ronald said nothing; he flung himself from the room,
> flung himself upon his horse and rode madly off in all
> directions."
>
> Stephen B Leacock, in "Gertrude the Governess: or Simple
> Seventeen", one of his *Nonsense Novels*.

5    "Sarah had only her school French, which was fine
     for reading Victor Hugo"

> Victor-Marie Hugo (1802-1885), French writer, whose
> works include *Les Misérables* and *Notre-Dame de Paris*
> ("The Hunchback of Notre-Dame"), both of which are
> frequently assigned-reading in French classes in English-
> Canadian schools.

## Chapter 2 – Mulled Wine by the Fireplace

9    "This year no stockings had been 'hung by the
     chimney with care'."

> "Twas the night before Christmas,
>     when all through the house
> Not a creature was stirring, not even a mouse;
> The stockings were all hung by the chimney with care,
> In hopes that St. Nicholas soon would be there"
>
> Clement Clarke Moore, *A Visit from St Nicolas*
> (a k a 'The Night Before Christmas')

11   "the wedding feast in Cana"

> Bible, John 2:1–11

12   "Contentment is the only real wealth".

> The author has been unable to trace the source of this
> quotation, which is widely attributed to Alfred Nobel,
> Swedish industrialist and founder of the Nobel Prizes.

## Chapter 3 – Theology in the Annexe

19    "Did that God create the world in 6 days and take a
      rest on the 7th, as described in the Christian Bible?"

      Bible, Genesis 1:1–31, 2:1–3.

21    "... the Christian Church would be built on sand"

      *Bible,* Matthew 7:26

21    "his reference to Jesus being both God and Man—and
      for that matter also the Son of  God and the Son of
      Man—simply referred this unsolved mystery to
      another one, that of the Trinity."

      John was not the first person to find these concepts difficult
      to comprehend. So many "Christological heresies" had arisen
      in the first centuries of Christendom, that the Council of
      Chalcedon was held in 451 to pronounce the orthodoxy that
      in Christ the two natures, the Divine and the human, each
      retaining its own properties, are united in one subsistence
      and one person. Theologians refer to this as the **Hypostatic
      Union.**

      If we add in a third person, the Holy Spirit (or "Holy
      Ghost"), we get the **Trinity**. In the words of the Athanasian
      Creed: "the Father is God, the Son is God, and the Holy
      Spirit is God, and yet there are not three Gods but one God."

      It is tempting to speculate that adding the Son of God and the
      Son of Man (both of whom are frequently mentioned in the
      New Testament) to this mix, bringing the total number of
      personages to five, might result in the *Quintessential Union.*
      But theologians seem to have decided that three is the
      optimal number of figures in the Godhead. The reasoning
      may be that the two Sons can be regarded as mere nicknames
      for Jesus.

      Any reader wishing to pursue this further is referred to *The
      Catholic Encyclopedia*, which contains vast amounts of
      discussion on this topic.

25   "Jesus did, after all, tell his disciples to love one another as he had loved them."

> "A new commandment I give unto you, That ye love one another; as I have loved you, that ye also love one another." *Bible,* John 13:34. This is sometimes referred to as the *mandatum novum* (the new commandment), and it is from this that Maundy Thursday (the day before Good Friday) gets its name.

## Chapter 4 – A Second Christmas Dinner

31   "Jesus loves me, this I know; for the Bible tells me so"

> These are the first two lines of a hymn, with music by William B Bradbury and words by Anna B Warner, which probably everyone who has ever attended Sunday school has sung at some point.

32   "a God whom *no one* has ever seen"

> "No man hath seen God at any time" *Bible,* John 1:18; 1 John 4:12
>
> The above quotation, which occurs in the Gospel and one of the Epistles of John, is generally attributed to the apostle John. This poses a problem for thoughtful believers, since Christian dogma insists that Jesus—as part of the "Godhead", or Trinity—*is* God, and John would have seen Jesus on many occasions.
>
> Is it possible that John means that no one has seen God *the father*, whereas many people have seen God *the son*? No, it isn't. The Greek word used by John in both of the above places to describe the person whom no one has ever seen is θεον (*theos*, meaning 'God'), not πατρος (*pater*, meaning 'father'), which John uses in a number of places to refer to God the father. In fact, one of those places is in the continuation of the first of the above passages:
>
> "No man hath seen God (*theos*) at any time, the only begotten Son, which is in the bosom of the Father (*pater*), he hath declared him." *Bible,* John 1:18
>
> Here John clearly distinguishes Jesus ('the Son', whom he has seen on many occasions) from God.

32    "On the contrary, it states that God has created us
      humans 'in his own image' ..."

> *Bible,* Genesis 1:26–27
>
> For the full Biblical text of, and comment on, this passage
> see the Notes to Chapter 13.

32    " ... which—if it means anything—must mean that
      God has endowed us with some of his own
      attributes."

> It is tantalizing to reflect that one of the divine attributes with
> which God has endowed us might be the ability to create
> things in our own image—such as gods.

33    "Onward Faithless Soldiers"

> This is a reference to hymn no. 391 in *Hymns Ancient and
> Modern*, the well-known "Onward Christian Soldiers", with
> words by Rev Sabine Baring-Gould (1834–1924), a noted
> folklorist, and music by Sir Arthur Sullivan (1842–1900)
> who wrote the music to the Gilbert and Sullivan operas.

35    "a little more than a little is by much too much"

> "They surfeited with honey and began
> To loathe the taste of sweetness, whereof a little
> More than a little is by much too much."
>
> Shakespeare, King *Henry IV*, part 1, act III, scene 2

37    "the term 'joyful noise' in Psalm 100"

> "Make a joyful noise unto the LORD, all ye lands.
> Serve the LORD with gladness: come before his presence
> with singing."
>
> *Bible*, Psalm 100:1–2

37    "Why should the Devil have all the good music?"

> The origin of this quotation is probably forever concealed in
> the mists of time. Amongst the many people to whom it has
> been attributed are:
>
> Martin Luther (1483–1546), Protestant reformer
> John Wesley (1703–1791), co-founder of Methodism and
> publisher of hymn tunes

William Booth (1829–1912), co-founder of the Salvation
Army

## Chapter 5 – A Walk Under the Stars

40    "The Big Bang Theory—ironically, proposed by a
Roman Catholic priest"

> Georges Henri Joseph Éduard Lemaître (1894–1966) was a
> Belgian Roman Catholic priest and  professor of physics who
> proposed what became known as the Big Bang theory of the
> origin of the Universe, which he called his 'Hypothesis of the
> Primeval Atom', in the pages of *Nature* in 1931.

42    *"Le coeur a ses raisons que la raison ne connaît
point"*

> ["The heart has its reasons, which reason does not know"]
> Blaise Pascal (1623–1662), French mathematician, physicist
> and philosopher, *Pensées* [*Thoughts*]

42    "As far as I can make out, Jesus' main message was
that we should love one another"

> "A new commandment I give unto you, That ye love one
> another; as I have loved you, that ye also love one another."
> *Bible,* John 13:34. (See notes to Chapter 3.)

43    "Is that not a contradictory folly?"

> The *Bible* contains many contradictions. For example:
>
> - In the first chapter of Genesis, God first creates the plants
>   then, on subsequent days, the (non-human) animals,  and
>   finally, man (Gen 1:11–28). In the second chapter of
>   Genesis, man is created first, followed by the plants, then
>   the remaining animals (Gen 2:7–20).
>
> - God warns Adam not to eat the fruit "of the tree of the
>   knowledge of good and evil" because "in the day that
>   thou eatest thereof thou shalt surely die" (Gen 2:17).
>   Adam disobeys God (Gen. 3:6), eats the forbidden fruit,
>   and lives to the ripe old age of 930 (Gen. 5:5). (However,
>   Adam does get thrown out of the Garden of Eden.)
>
> - "I will dash them one against another, even the fathers
>   and the sons together, saith the LORD: I will not pity, nor

spare, nor have mercy, but destroy them" (Jeremiah 13:14).

"The LORD is good to all: and his tender mercies are over all his works" (Psalm 145:9).

- According to Matthew, Joseph fled with Mary and their new-born son from Bethlehem, where Jesus was born, to Egypt. There they stayed until the death of Herod, who had decreed that all children under the age of two should be put to death, hoping in this way to kill Jesus (Matt 2:13–15).

  According to Luke, from Bethlehem Mary and Joseph brought Jesus "to Jerusalem, to present him to the Lord" (Luke 2:22), after which, "when they had performed all things according to the law of the Lord, they returned into Galilee, to their own city Nazareth" (Luke 2:39). There is no mention in Luke of any infanticide or flight to Egypt.

- The genealogy of Jesus in Mathew 1:1–16 lists 42 generations from Joseph (Jesus' non-father) to David (inclusive). This same period in Luke 3:23–34, covers 55 generations, with only a few ancestors appearing in both lists. Ignoring the inconsistency of names, we can estimate that the difference of 13 generations corresponds to a discrepancy of about 325 years, allowing 25 years per generation.

  The Luke genealogy goes on (Luke 3:34–38) for another 21 generations, tracing Jesus' ancestry all the way back to Adam, and from him to God. Again assuming 25 years per generation, this would mean that the earth was created approximately 3900 years ago [(55 + 21) * 25 + 2000 = 3900].

  However, our calculations fail to take into account that men in Old Testament times were apparently made of sterner stuff than modern man. According to Genesis, Adam was 130 when he gave birth to Seth, who in turn was 105 when he gave birth to Enos. Methuselah was all of 187 when he gave birth to Lamech, who was 182 when he gave birth to Noah (who built the ark). Noah seems to have been 502 when he gave birth to Shem. And so on. (Gen 5:1–32)

  Taking the longer generational spans of these Patriarchs into account, Young Earth Creationists (YECs) have calculated that the world is 6,000–10,000 years old.

- Luke 1:26–35 claims that Mary was a virgin when she conceived, making the foregoing genealogies of Joseph (who was thus not Jesus' father) irrelevant.

- According to the Gospel of John (19:17), Jesus carried his own cross all the way to Golgotha ("the place of a skull"). However, according to the other three Gospels (Mathew, Mark and Luke)—which are frequently referred to as the *synoptic gospels*, because they share a common view ('synoptic' means 'together seeing' in Greek), and probably a common origin—Simon of Cyrenia carried the cross for Jesus (Matthew 27:32, Mark 15:21, Luke 23:26).

The *Bible* contains a large number of such contradictions, in both the Old and the New Testaments. However, John did not waste his time discussing these with Yvette, because all of them are **non-essential contradictions**, that is the contradiction exists between different statements about a thing, not in the nature (or 'essence') of the thing itself. In all such cases, it is possible to select *one* of the statements, proclaim it to be the truth, and then say that the other statements contain errors introduced by human scribes. (Or to engage in theological hocus-pocus to show that there is "really" no contradiction at all.)

The divine/human nature of Christ, however, which John *did* take up, is an **essential contradiction**. This is a contradiction that is built into the essence of the thing being discussed. It occurs when we claim that a thing both possesses and does not posses a certain property. For example, a square circle claims that the thing is both round and not round at the same time. A stone too heavy for God to lift would require God to be both omnipotent (in order to create the stone) and not omnipotent (since he can't lift it) at the same time.

It is in the nature of humanness not to be God. Unless God possesses qualities that humans do not, he can no more create universes than you or I can. If Jill is a human, she is *necessarily* not God. The same applies to any other human, even if his name happens to be Jesus. To claim that Jesus is both God and human, as is done in the doctrines of the **Hypostatic Union** and the **Trinity** (see Notes on Chapter 4), is to claim that he is both God and not God. At the same time.

The system of logical thinking upon which the whole of Western science and philosophy is based, does not accept as valid any system which allows contradictions, whether essential or non-essential. The reason for this is that **in any system which contains a contradiction, it is possible to prove anything**.

Consider, for example, a system which accepts the following two statements as true:

1. The world is flat.

2. The world is not flat.

Then by a fundamental theorem of logic, called Addition, it follows from 1 that

3. The world is flat OR I am a poached egg.

(What the *Addition Theorem* says, is that if we know that a given statement is true, then it follows that at least one of the pair of statements, consisting of the given statement and *any* other statement, must be true.)

But by 2, the world is not flat. Therefore, by another fundamental theorem of logic, called Denial of a Disjunct, we have no choice but to deduce from 2 and 3 that

4. I am a poached egg.

(What the *Denial of a Disjunct Theorem* says, is that if we know that at least one of a pair of statements is true, and we know that one of them is false, then we are justified in concluding that the remaining statement of the pair is true.)

It should be obvious that *any* statement and its contradiction could be substituted for 1 and 2 above, and that they, in turn, could be used to prove *any* statement in place of 4.

There are many ways of proving the same thing in modern logic. The author has chosen this somewhat old-fashioned proof, because it doesn't presuppose any knowledge of formal logic on the part of the reader.

As an exercise, the interested reader could try substituting the statement "Jesus is God." and its contradiction for 1 and 2 above, then using them to prove that the world is 5 days old.

There are few, if any, other matters on which human minds have tied themselves up in so many knots as has been the case with the question of the supposed divinity of Jesus.

Anyone interested in pursuing this idea further, might begin by reading the article on 'Christology' in *The Catholic Encyclopedia.*

The author would like to point out that the foregoing does not imply any disrespect for Jesus as a person, or as a teacher. But it does heap scorn on the notion, imposed on him by later-day theologians, that Jesus was God—at any rate if by God we mean a supernatural being who has created the universe.

## 44    "The Bible tells us that God knew beforehand that Jesus would fulfil the Biblical prophesies about a Messiah"

"And the angel said unto her, Fear not, Mary: for thou hast found favour with God.

"And, behold, thou shalt conceive in thy womb, and bring forth a son, and shalt call his name JESUS.

"He shall be great, and shall be called the Son of the Highest: and the Lord God shall give unto him the throne of his father David:

"And he shall reign over the house of Jacob for ever; and of his kingdom there shall be no end."

*Bible*, Luke 1:30–33

## 44    "which necessarily required him to live a sinless life"

A question that has furrowed the brows of the world's theologians for almost 2000 years is that of Jesus' **sinlessness**. Councils have been held and many books written on this subject. The Bible itself, surprisingly, has very little to say on the matter. There seem to be only three verses which refer to Christ's sinlessness, two directly ("in him is no sin" – 1 John 3:5; "Christ ... did no sin, neither was guile found in his mouth" – 1 Peter 2:21–22), and the third obliquely ("For he hath made him to be sin for us, who knew no sin; that we might be made the righteousness of God in him." – 2 Corinthians 5:21. If you don't understand the third quotation, you are not alone! Many learned treatises have been written, trying to elucidate this verse.)

*The Catholic Encyclopedia* says "The fact that Christ never sinned is an article of faith ... The impossibility of a sinful act by Christ is taught by all theologians, but variously explained." A number of arguments are brought up, perhaps the most ingenious of which is the observation that if Jesus, in his human role, were to sin, he would be sinning against himself in his role as God, which is dismissed as "absolutely impossible".

44    "At any rate, not according to the Bible, which says we are all sinners in need of forgiveness."

> "For all have sinned, and come short of the glory of God"
>
> *Bible*, Romans 3:23
>
> "If we say that we have no sin, we deceive ourselves, and the truth is not in us."
>
> *Bible*, I John 1:8
>
> At various times and places, claiming to be without sin has itself been considered  a sin, based on such verses as I John 1:10: "If we say that we have not sinned, we make Him a liar, and His word is not in us."

44    "Even the Lord's prayer assumes that we need forgiveness for our sins."

> There are a number of different versions of the Lord's Prayer. Here is one taken straight out of the *Bible*:
>
> "Our Father which art in heaven, Hallowed be thy name.
> Thy kingdom come. Thy will be done, as in heaven, so in earth.
> Give us day by day our daily bread.
> And forgive us our sins;
> for we also forgive every one that is indebted to us.
> And lead us not into temptation; but deliver us from evil."
>
> *Bible,* (Luke 11: 2–4):

## Chapter 6 – Morning in the Cottage

50    "But now I have the opportunity to become a **bride of Christ**."

> The term "bride of Christ" does not appear in the Bible. There are, however, a few biblical passages in the New Testament which appear to liken the "church" itself (i e the whole body of worshipers), to the bride of Christ. The following list is believed to be exhaustive. The comments within square brackets have been inserted by the author.

*2 Corinthians 11:2.* "... I have espoused you [believers] to one husband, that I may present you as a chaste virgin to Christ"

*Ephesians 5:22-27.* "... For the husband is the head of the wife, even as Christ is the head of the church ..."

*Revelation 19:6-9.* "... for the marriage of the Lamb is come, and his wife [the body of faithful believers] hath made herself ready ... Blessed are they which are called unto the marriage supper of the Lamb ..."

*Revelation 21:1-2.* "...Jerusalem ... prepared as a bride adorned for her husband."

*Revelation 21:9.* "... I will shew thee **the bride, the Lamb's wife**."

At a very early date the church fathers adopted the practice of consecrating virgins (*consecratio virginum*), whom they referred to as "Brides of Christ". During the ceremony for consecrating virgins in the **Roman Pontifical** (*Pontificale Romanum*), the nun's veil is handed over with these words: "Receive the sacred veil, that thou mayst be known to have despised the world, and to be truly, humbly, and with all thy heart subject to **Christ as His bride**; and may He defend thee from all evil, and bring thee to life eternal." (The *Roman Pontifical* is a book of liturgy used by Roman Catholic bishops. Early versions dating from the first millennium of the Christian church exist in manuscript form.)

Current Catholic orthodoxy on this subject is contained in the **Encyclical on Consecrated Virginity** (*Sacra Virginitas*) promulgated by Pope Pius XII on March 25, 1954, from which the following extracts are taken. (The bracketed numbers are references to footnotes in the Encyclical. The unbracketed numbers are paragraph numbers in that document.)

"HOLY VIRGINITY and that perfect chastity which is consecrated to the service of God is without doubt among the most precious treasures which the Founder of the Church has left in heritage to the society which He established ...

"17. Moreover the Fathers of the Church considered this obligation of perfect chastity as a kind of **spiritual marriage**, in which **the soul is wedded to Christ** ... Thus, St. Athanasius writes that the Catholic Church has been accustomed to call those who have the virtue of virginity the

**spouses of Christ**.[23] And St. Ambrose, writing succinctly of the consecrated virgin, says, 'She is a virgin who is **married to God**.'[24] In fact, ... as early as the fourth century the rite of consecration of a virgin was very like the rite the Church uses in our own day in the marriage blessing.[26]

"18. For the same reason the Fathers exhort virgins to love their **Divine Spouse** more ardently than they would love a husband ... thus St. Methodius ... 'You yourself, O Christ, are my all. For you I keep myself chaste, and holding aloft my shining lamp I run to meet you, **my Spouse**.'[30] ... Certainly it is the love of Christ that urges a virgin to retire behind convent walls and remain there all her life, in order to contemplate and love **the heavenly Spouse** more easily and without hindrance;"

The Encyclical (§65) makes it clear that the Roman Catholic church's obsession with virginity has its origins in Mary, the mother of Jesus, who according to the New Testament was a virgin when she conceived (although the precise details of how this was accomplished are somewhat sketchy). There are two accounts of the virgin birth: Matthew 1:28–25 (which quotes an Old-Testament prophesy contained in Isaiah 7:14) and Luke 1:26–38.

It is somewhat embarrassing for the Roman Catholic authorities that the New Testament contains several explicit references to Jesus' brothers and sisters (eg Matthew 13:55-56, Mark 6:3, Galatians 1:19). However, after a virtuosic display of theological logic-chopping, the *Catholic Encyclopedia*, in its article "The Brethren of the Lord", comes to the conclusion that the "brethren" named in the New Testament were "neither the brothers nor the step-brothers of the Lord". (There does not seem to be any corresponding treatment of "The Sisters of the Lord".)

The same article is at pains to tell us that the references to Jesus being Mary's "firstborn son" (Matthew 1:25, Luke 2:7) do *not* mean that she had any other sons. Neither do the words "'he [Joseph, Mary's husband] knew her not till she brought forth' [Matthew 1:25] imply ... that he knew her afterwards". The "perpetual virginity of Our Blessed Lady" (i e the idea that Mary remained a virgin despite her marriage to Joseph) is a dogma of the Roman Catholic Church, which is expounded in numerous places in the *Catholic*

*Encyclopedia* (e g in the articles "Virgin Birth of Christ" and "The Blessed Virgin Mary: Mary's perpetual virginity"). This dogma does not seem to have any scriptural basis (and is, indeed, rejected by many other Christian denominations). It is instead based on appeals to early church authorities. But that is another discussion.

53    "Mr van Winkle"

Rip van Winkle is the main character in a story of the same name published in 1819 by the American author Washington Irving (1783–1859). Mr van Winkle is renowned for falling asleep under a tree and waking up 20 years later. One event that he missed out on during his long slumber was the American War of Independence (1775–1783).

55    "We have erred and strayed from thy ways like lost sheep ... and there is no health in us ... have mercy upon us miserable offenders"

From the General Confession (Morning and Evening Prayer) in *The Book of Common Prayer*

## Chapter 7 – The Walk to Fletcher's

59    "fallen down a rabbit hole"

This is how Alice got into Wonderland in Lewis Carroll's (pen name of Charles Dodgson) immortal children's story *Alice's Adventures in Wonderland*

59    "miniature sleigh and eight tiny reindeer"

"When what to my wondering eyes should appear,
But a miniature sleigh and eight tiny reindeer."

Clement Clarke Moore, *A Visit from St Nicola*
(a k a 'The Night Before Christmas')

59    "Could enough monkeys with their typewriters, even working in shifts around the clock, really produce the works of Shakespeare by accident, given enough time?"

The *Infinite Monkey Theorem* has a long history. Variations go back to Aristotle, but the modern version was introduced in 1913 by French mathematician Émile Borel. Statistically, given an infinite number of monkeys, or an infinite amount of time, the answer is yes.

However, to put it into perspective, just to produce the single phrase "To be or not to be" (18 characters, including spaces), would require "on average" either 1,000,000,000,000,000,000,000,000,000,000,000,000 monkeys (36 zeros) each making 18 random key strokes, or one monkey doing it that many times, or some intermediate number of monkeys collectively making that number of attempts.

The reasoning is as follows. Assume a typewriter with 50 printing keys and one shift key (i e 100 characters to choose from), then the chances that a random key stroke will produce 'T' are $1/100$, which is equal to $(1/10)^2$. The chances that two random strokes will produce 'To' are therefore $1/100$ x $1/100$, or $(1/10)^4$. Thus the chances that 18 random strokes will produce the whole phrase are $(1/10)^{36}$.

A team of 3 monkeys working in shifts around the clock at the rate of 116 attempts (116 x 18 random keystrokes) per hour would make 1,000,000 ($10^6$) attempts per year.

If we assigned 3 billion (3 x $10^9$) such teams (9 billion monkeys, slightly more than the current human population of the world) to the task, it would take them "on average" about 3 x $10^{20}$ years to come up with that single 18-character phrase from one of Shakespeare's works. This is more than 200,000,000,000 (2 x $10^{11}$) *times* the estimated age of the universe (which is 13.7 billion years).

Nevertheless, the fact remains that theoretically—given an infinite amount of time—it would be possible for one of the monkeys to produce the complete works of Shakespeare. In fact—theoretically—he could do it on his first attempt!

60    "You mean the way Satan tempted Jesus in the wilderness?"

*Bible,* Matthew 4:1–11.

60    "fast for 40 days and 40 nights"

*Bible,* Matthew 4:2

62    "Get thee behind me, Satan"

*Bible,* Matthew 16:23

63    "I the LORD thy God am a jealous God, visiting the
      iniquity of the fathers upon the children unto the third
      and fourth generation of them that hate me."

> Bible, Exodus 20:5 (The Ten Commandments)

66    "*Je n'en sçay rien, mais m'actend du tout à Notre-
      Seigneur.*"

> ["I do not know; but in everything I commit myself to God."]
>
> Le Procès de Jeanne d'Arc, Cinquième interrogatoire secret,
> 14 mars 1431.

67    Galileo

> Galileo Galilei (1564–1642)

## Chapter 8 – Fletcher's General Store

71    Norman Rockwell (1894–1978). American painter
      and illustrator.

> Rockwell is most famous for the (often humorous) cover
> illustrations of everyday-life situations he painted for *The
> Saturday Evening Post* magazine over more than four
> decades. Many of the scenarios he painted were nostalgic
> even when they first appeared.

73    "When people stop believing in God, they don't
      believe in nothing, they believe in anything"

> The author has been unable to find the source of this
> quotation, which is widely attributed to G K Chesterton
> (1874– 1936), writer, journalist, philosopher and many other
> things, perhaps best known today as the author of the Father
> Brown stories.

74    "divine coprolites waiting to be analysed by some
      future palaeontologist"

> 'Coprolite' is a fancy name for fossilized faeces, although, if
> the truth be told, neither of these terms was the one that
> actually went through John's mind—something that may
> have contributed to his feeling of irreverence.

76    "He that is unmarried careth for the things that belong
      to the Lord ... But he that is married careth for the
      things that are of the world."

      *Bible,* 1 Corinthians 7:32–33

77    "be tormented with fire and brimstone ... for ever and
      ever"

      *Bible,* Revelations 14:10–11

## Chapter 9 - The Walk Home

79    "... all three major monotheistic religions revere as
      one of their founding fathers, a man who was
      prepared to slit the throat of his own son, because he
      thought he had heard a voice telling him to do so."

      The story of how Abraham was prepared to sacrifice his son
      Isaac is told in the *Bible,* Genesis 22:1-18. Many Muslims
      consider that it was Abraham's first son, Ishmael (by the
      Egyptian slave Hagar), not his second son, Isaac (by his wife
      Sarah), whose throat Abraham was prepared to slit. The
      Koran itself, in telling this story (sura 37:99–111), does not
      name the son.

80    "a house built on sand."

      *Bible,* Matthew 7:26

81    "conversion, like that of Saul on the road to
      Damascus"

      *Bible,* Acts 9: 1–20

81    "light from heaven"

      *Bible,* Acts 9:3

81    "a lake of fire"

      *Bible,* Revelations 19:20

81　"Verily, verily, what man hath joined together, God
　　hath put asunder."

> The reference is to the formula "Those whom God hath
> joined together, let no man put asunder", from the Marriage
> ceremony in *The Book of Common Prayer.*

83　"According to the Bible Jesus was without sin."

> Regarding Jesus' sinlessness, see notes on Chapter 5.

83　"God is love"

> *Bible,* 1 John 4:16

85　"live together after God's ordinance in the holy estate
　　of matrimony"

> Marriage ceremony in The Book of Common Prayer

## Chapter 10 – The Abbey Church & Drive Back

97　"During the second world war, an attempt to
　　assassinate Hitler came very close to succeeding."

> Numerous plots to assassinate Hitler, before and during the
> Second World War, have come to light, and there were
> probably others that we shall never know about.
>
> However, only one of these plots seems to have come close
> to succeeding. On the 20th of July, 1944, Colonel Claus von
> Stauffenberg placed a bomb with a time fuse under the
> conference table at which Hitler was sitting with some
> German officers. The bomb detonated, demolishing the
> conference room and killing several of those present, but
> Hitler himself escaped with only minor injuries—and the
> indignity of having his trousers blown off.
>
> Stauffenberg and thousands of suspected plotters and
> sympathizers were ruthlessly hunted down. About 200 of
> them were executed.
>
> As a sincere catholic, Stauffenberg had a long struggle with
> his conscience before he was able to convince himself that it
> was morally justified for him to kill one man in order to save
> thousands—or even millions—of others.

It is almost inconceivable that he would *not* have asked God for help in his mission. And it *is* inconceivable that none of the other believers in Germany would have prayed for God to intervene and rid their country of its murderous tyrant. Yet God seems to have ignored these prayers and instead answered those of Hitler's supporters. If he intervened at all.

It was almost certainly this incident that John was referring to.

97    "Ours not to reason why, ours but to do and die"

"Theirs not to reason why, Theirs but to do and die"

Alfred, Lord Tennyson, The Charge of the Light Brigade:

## Chapter 11 – Christmas Presents

103    "Thou shalt not bear false witness"

*Bible,* Exodus 20:16, etc (The Ten Commandments)

## Chapter 12 – Dinner with Helen's Family

113    "the Seven Dwarfs might today be remembered for singing whilst they worked, instead of whistling"

An allusion to the Walt Disney film *Snow White and the Seven Dwarfs*, which contained the song *Whistle While You Work.*

113    "I'm dreaming of a white Christmas"

Written by Irving Berlin, this is one of several much-loved Christmas carols written by Jewish composers and song-writers. Others include *Let it snow! Let it snow! Let it snow!,* *Silver Bells* and *Rockin' Around the Christmas Tree.*

115    "the Koran, tells them in no uncertain terms that they must not rest until the entire world has been conquered for Islam"

*Koran,* sura 2:193; sura 8:39; sura 9:29, 33, 123; etc

115   "It also warns them not to befriend Christians or Jews"

> *Koran*, sura 3:28, 118–120; sura 4:101, 144; sura 5:51, 80; sura 58:14–22; sura 60:1; etc

115   "and explicitly tells them that Jesus was *not* the son of God."

> *Koran*, sura 3:59; sura 4:171; sura 5:17, 73, 75, 116; sura 6:101; sura 9:30–31; sura 10:68; sura 18:4–5; sura 19:35, 88–92; sura 43:57–59; etc

116   "it is a dogma of Muslim faith that every word in the Koran has been dictated by God himself"

> Muslims believe that the *Koran* (or *Qur'an*, as it is often spelt) is the literal, verbal communication of God [suras 10:37; 11:13–14; 69:40–43; etc] and that it is a transcript of *The Eternal Book* written by God himself and safeguarded by him in one of his heavens [suras 43:4; 56:77–80, etc]. They believe that God sent the angel Gabriel [sura 2:97; etc] to reveal parts of the *Koran* to Muhammad as the need arose [suras 17:106; 25:32; etc]. *Qur'an* in Arabic means "the recitation" (i.e. of God's own words).
>
> Muslims believe it is significant that God revealed the *Koran* in Arabic [suras 12:2; 20:113; 26:195; etc] "without any crookedness" [sura 39:28] (i.e. free from ambiguity). Therefore whenever passages from the *Koran* are read in mosques—even in countries where the population does not speak Arabic—it is always read from an Arabic *Koran*.
>
> In fact, many (especially Arab) Muslims consider that the *Koran* is untranslatable, that it ceases to be the word of God once it is no longer couched in the Arabic language. For this reason a number of (comparatively modern) translations have been called *The Meaning of the Koran* or *The Message of the Qur'an*, etc, implying that if you want to read the "real" *Koran*, you will have to learn Arabic.
>
> (Male) children who don't (initially) understand a word of Arabic are taught to memorize the entire Arabic *Koran* (roughly half the length of the New Testament) in religious schools or madrasas. Someone who has achieved this prodigious feat is called a *hafiz*. The 1400-year old Arabic of the *Koran* is still held up as an ideal for—especially

written—Arabic today, since it is considered to be—quite literally—the language of God.

## 116    "Islam is totally incompatible with Christianity"

Many verses from the *Koran,* which clearly illustrate this incompatibility, have been listed above.

While the *Koran* is considered to be the literal word of God—not that of Muhammad, who is described as God's Messenger—some of the utterances of Muhammad himself have been collected in various volumes of *Hadith,* considered to be second only to the *Koran* in authority. (Muhammad himself was reportedly illiterate [*Koran* suras 7:157, 62:2; *Bukhari* 8:194; *Muslim* 6:2376, 41:7000, etc] and therefore did not leave any written records.) One saying of Muhammad, which is recorded more than once in the *Hadith,* is this: "I have been commanded to fight people until they testify that there is no god but Allah and that Muhammad is the Messenger of Allah ..." [*Sahih Muslim* 1:30–33]

*Sharia Law* is based primarily on the *Koran* and *Hadith.* According to Sharia Law, "to deny any verse of the Koran or anything which by scholarly consensus belongs to it" is considered to be apostasy [*Umdat al-Salik* o8.7(7)] and is punishable by death [*ibid* f1.3, o8.2, o8.4]. Another act which is considered apostasy (and subject to the same penalty) is belief in the acceptability of non-Islamic religions [*ibid* o8.7(20)].

Lawyers generally enjoy arguing about the finer points of law, and in this regard Islamic lawyers are no exception. The above quotations (from *Umdat al-Salik*) are from one of the four Sunni schools of Islamic Law (the Shafi'i school). However, it is estimated that these four schools agree on 75% of their legal conclusions, and agreement is probably even greater when it comes to what constitutes *kufr* (unbelief) and *ridda* (apostasy). Even the Shia schools would probably agree with the foregoing conclusions. It is highly unlikely that any school of Sharia Law could be found that would find non-Islamic religions acceptable.

## Chapter 13 – A Last Walk Under the Stars

120    "becoming the Bride of Christ"

> See notes on Chapter 6.

120    "the Second Coming, perhaps"

> The return of Christ to judge mankind is referred to in many
> biblical passages, such as:
>
> *Bible,* Matthew 24:27, 25:31, Acts 10:42, 17:31, etc

124    "They will not have a spirit, which comes from God"

> The idea that God breathed his spirit into his creation, man,
> derives from such passages as:
>
> *Bible,* Genesis 2:7, Exodus 31:3, Job 33:4, etc

124    "Only man has been created in God's image"

> The idea that (wo)man has been created in God's image
> comes from this biblical passage:
>
> "And God said, Let us make man in our image, after our
> likeness: and let them have dominion over the fish of the sea,
> and over the fowl of the air, and over the cattle, and over all
> the earth, and over every creeping thing that creepeth upon
> the earth.
>
> "So God created man in his own image, in the image of God
> created he him; male and female created he them." *Bible,*
> Genesis 1:26–27
>
> The idea is confirmed—for males of the species—in *Bible,*
> 1 Corinthians 11:7. However, women get short shrift here,
> being described as "the glory of the man", rather than images
> of God.
>
> For a reflection on which divine attributes we may have been
> endowed with, see the Notes to Chapter 4.

125    "Weren't you about to instruct the devil to take up a
       position in the rear?"

> See "Get thee behind me, Satan" in notes to Chap 7.

## Chapter 14 – Breakfast, Cribbage and Lunch

127   "Schubert's G-flat Impromptu"

> Opus 90:3 (D 899)

128   "40 days in the wilderness"

> *Bible,* Matthew 4:1–2

134   *"Quisquis non receperit regnum Dei velut parvulus, non intrabit in illud."*

> ["Whosoever shall not receive the kingdom of God as a little child, he shall not enter therein."]
>
> *Bible,* Mark 10:15 (Vulgate)

## Chapter 15 – The Drive Back to Montreal

137   Moonlight Sonata

> Op 27:2 by Ludwig van Beethoven. The first movement is frequently one of the first pieces of classical music attempted by piano students.

137   Liebstraum No 3

> S.541:3 by Franz Liszt. This is considerably more difficult than (the first movement of) Moonlight Sonata, but is nevertheless frequently found in the repertoire of more advanced amateurs.

137   Copernicus

> Nicolaus Copernicus (1473–1543)

138   Galileo

> See notes on Chapter 7.

## Chapter Notes

These notes contain a reference to themselves.

www.ingramcontent.com/pod-product-compliance
Lightning Source LLC
Chambersburg PA
CBHW060746180626
46818CB00002B/472

*  9  7  8  9  1  6  3  3  4  2  9  7  4  *